The Vienna Trilogy

BOOK TWO

Nazis on the Run

by Tom Gilligan

Illustrations by Everett Walker

Intelligence e-Publishing Company
Cape Cod, Massachusetts

Intelligence Book Division

Intelligence e-Publishing Company, Cape Cod, Massachusetts

Illustrations by Everett Walker.

Book Design by Charles King (ckmm.com).

Cover image courtesy of Carl Weinrother
https://commons.wikimedia.org/wiki/File:Bundesarchiv_B_145_
Bild-P054320,_Berlin,_Brandenburger_Tor_und_Pariser_Platz.jpg

ISBN 978-0-9729659-4-1

Library of Congress Control Number: 2022914020

Contents

Prologue

World War II had come to an end in late summer 1945 when both Germany and Japan surrendered to the Allied Armies led by the United States and Great Britain who had entered into a treaty with Soviet Russia. It is believed that as many as 50 million people were killed in what became the greatest war in human history. The first two years after the war were a time of both great suffering and modest recovery from seven years of destruction and death. The first two years were also especially confusing, as Communists in both Europe and Asia, rather than seeking peaceful ways, launched their own programs of world conquest.

By mid-summer of 1947—as many European nations and millions of wandering refugees were still struggling to recover from World War II—eleven year old David Hale had just completed his first mission as a junior spy. He had recently helped his father rescue an important Polish scientist who was on the wrong side of the Danube River that separated East from West—the Soviet Russian from the American zone of Austria (*The Vienna Trilogy, Book One: Escape to the West*). At the time of this book, there were Nazi war criminals who wanted to escape to Latin America to pursue once again Adolf Hitler's dream of world conquest.

What could one boy do in the face of such dangerous enemies? Nazis, on the run, would soon find out.

Dedication

To all innocent souls who lost their freedom
to Nazism, Fascism and Imperialism
in World War II
—especially women, children
and the most vulnerable
unable to escape or fight back.

1

The Vogels

After trying without success to think of ways to get his dad to put his medical duties aside and get back to spying, David rolled out of bed. He descended to the first floor in his usual way—acrobatically, swiftly but silently. As he almost glided down the stairwell, he felt that, with a little more effort and practice, he might actually be able to fly. Dr. Matt Hale, David's dad, under no false *illusions,** was busy writing medical reports on his examination of Displaced Persons in the camps. Typhoid fever was becoming again a major problem. It was his job to get the problem *resolved.*†

The boy went into the study, made *eye contact*‡ with his father, said he had been thinking about things and had an idea. "What if I use some of my free time to improve my German, Dad? I admit that I have been *indifferent,*§ even lazy, when it comes to studying the language. That was BEFORE. However SINCE the rescue operation, I now see things differently."

His father did not respond right away, but let David go on— he could see the boy had something important on his mind.

"Dad, you know what I realized when you were in the Russian guard shack the other night? You know, when we had

---

* Illusions: Fantasies or unrealistic dreams.
† Resolved: Fixed, cured, taken care of.
‡ Eye contact: When two people are looking at each other at the same time.
§ Indifferent: Having no real desire or motivation.

Dr. Kaminski hidden in the trunk—hanging in there between a new life of freedom and getting captured by the Russians?" Without waiting for a response, David continued. "I could tell, Dad, it was your excellent German and Russian language skills that made all the difference in getting us away from there and getting Dr. Kaminski to safety. Well, I want to understand and speak German much, much better—so I can help in the future—so I won't mess things up because my German stinks."

"Darn good idea, Son, and I have a suggestion—why not spend some time each day studying and speaking German with Katrina? You have lots of free time, especially with Ellie away. As you have probably found already, it is not easy to *master** German. It is one of the more difficult languages to learn and to speak really well. *Frau*[†] Vogel would be happy to help. Because you're on vacation, let's not call it a class—maybe we'll just call it a *tutorial.*[‡] It'll be entirely up to you and Katrina when you work on your German."

David liked what he was hearing—"That is how school ought to be," he thought. Later that morning, Matt Hale spoke with Katrina Vogel and her husband, Konrad, an old friend of Matt's from the war. Konrad had been in the anti-Nazi Austrian Underground Army that fought against Hitler starting in 1938, when the Germans invaded Austria. He found himself *eventually* being hunted by the Nazi Secret Police and *Herr*[§] Vogel

---

*   Master: To learn something at a high skill level. In the case of language learning, it would mean being able to speak as well as a person born and raised in Austria or Germany.

†   Frau: Mrs., in German.

‡   Tutorial: A private class with one teacher and one student.

§   Herr Vogel: Means Mr. Vogel in German.

managed to escape to London where some 30,000 Austrian refugees were organizing to fight against Nazi Germany. Having been trained by the U.S. Army Intelligence in England, Konrad Vogel in 1943 was dropped by *parachute** into Western Austria, not far from Salzburg. This was also not far from Adolf Hitler's mountain homes in nearby Bavaria, Germany.

Hitler's mountain home, known as 'The Berghof,' was bought with money he received for the book he wrote while in prison in the 1920's—it was named *Mein Kampf*, or *My Struggle.*† Naturally, every Nazi had bought one or more copies of the Fuehrer's book so Hitler's book earned him a lot of money.

For his 50th birthday—April 20, 1939—the German Nazi Party built and gave Hitler an entirely separate and *breathtaking*‡ mile-high mountaintop *retreat.*§ They called it "Eagle's Nest." *Ironically,*⁋ the Nazi leader seldom visited his Eagle's Nest for a simple reason, which was one of Nazi Germany's best kept secrets. Unlike those *majestic*** eagles that soared high above the *Alps,*†† Adolf Hitler was afraid of high places.

---

*   Parachute: A silk or cloth umbrella-like device for jumping safely from a flying airplane to the ground.

†   *Mein Kampf* (*My Struggle*): Hitler's own hate-filled explanation for his Nazi plan to restore Germany's lost powers from their defeat in World War I.

‡   Breathtaking: Something so striking that it would be said to take one's breath away with its beauty.

§   Retreat: A place for rest and relaxation.

⁋   Ironically: Where reality goes against the words used to describe it— the Nazis saw Hitler as an "eagle" but he was, in reality, *afraid of high places*. Irony is often used in a humorous way.

** Majestic: Considered grand and noble, the eagle is king of the bird world just as the lion is king of the jungle due to its great strength.

†† Alps: European mountain range that runs through Germany, Switzerland, Austria, France and Italy.

In the closing two years of the war, Konrad Vogel was kept busy fighting the German Army. He communicated, or sent back his secret messages to the U.S. Military Headquarters that were located outside London. Using a *shortwave radio*,* Vogel reported on Nazi *troop movements*.† He engaged in *sabotage operations*‡—blowing up bridges, roads and electric power stations. Konrad in the war was a genuine Austrian war hero—but a silent and secret one known only to the American Military. After the war ended, he returned to Vienna and to having the simple life as a carpenter and furniture maker. Except for Matt Hale, none of his neighbors in Vienna knew of Konrad Vogel's anti-Nazi wartime activities.

Besides improving David's German language skills, Matt Hale saw an added benefit in his son spending time each day with the Vogels—it might help the boy stay out of trouble. When Dr. Hale left the castle to visit and treat sick refugees throughout Eastern Austria, he could not take David along. He did not want to expose his son to any of the *communicable diseases*§ that existed among the foreign refugees. To keep from catching and spreading diseases, the doctors and nurses working in the camps had to wear *protective sanitary garments*.⁋

---

*   Shortwave radio: A machine that sends and receives messages over long distances, thousands of miles in fact because of the kind of radio wave it uses. It is, really, a perfect machine for spies working far away in enemy areas.

†   Troop movements: The movement of soldiers and equipment to fight battles.

‡   Sabotage operations: Blowing up and destroying tunnels and bridges, cutting electric power lines, and destroying German Army military equipment and supplies.

§   Communicable diseases: Diseases easily passed on to other people by contact, such as typhoid fever, pneumonia, tuberculosis, and the worst post-war disease—typhus.

⁋   Protective sanitary garments: Working clothes and uniforms that were free of germs and diseases.

Dr. Hale also wore this equipment, for he had no intention of becoming another *Typhoid Mary*.*

It was agreed, then, that David would spend part of his mornings with Katrina. After lunch, however, David and Thor would be entirely free to explore the castle itself as well as the castle *grounds*† until the doctor returned in the late afternoon or early evening. It would be during this free time in the afternoon that he would encounter the *intelligence trove*‡ at the center of his second spy operation.

David's German teacher Katrina was quite pleased that the boy was finally taking learning the language seriously. Katrina Vogel was a remarkable woman—more so than her *humble*§ manner would suggest. During the war, this very proper woman was a member of the secret '*O5 Austrian Resistance Organization*'¶ which fought bravely against the Nazi *occupiers*.** Late in the war, Katrina had assisted *downed*†† American pilots and *flight crews*‡‡ to escape being captured by the Nazis and

---

*   Typhoid Mary: A cook in the first part of the 20th century in the States, she is believed to have infected hundreds of people with typhoid fever that she carried in her body but which did not make her sick.
†   Grounds: The land all around the castle.
‡   Trove: A treasure or valuable collection that is found hidden somewhere.
§   Humble manner: Acting in a simple way that does not call attention to oneself.
¶   O5 Resistance Organization: Of the 100,000 Austrians who fought in the underground or resistance, O5 was the main group opposing German Nazi occupation.
** Occupiers: The people who invade and take over a country.
†† Downed: Those who had been shot down in the airplanes over Austria.
‡‡ Flight crews: On every Allied four-engine bomber there were as many as ten men who were all crew members, including the pilot who flew the airplane. There was a co-pilot, a navigator who chose the flight route they would take, a bombardier who dropped the bombs on enemy factories, dams and military targets, and men who fired the machine guns at attacking enemy fighter airplanes.

helped them work their way back to England, usually through Italy or Switzerland.

As with so many who risked their lives to help others live in freedom, Katrina Vogel never spoke of her wartime *exploits*.* She never got a medal for her bravery. There were no parades for those like her and Konrad who worked in the shadows against the German invaders. This *heroic*† couple did what was dangerous and right for a simple reason and a simple *code of conduct*‡—fighting against the German Nazis was the correct thing for any *patriotic*§ Austrian to do.

---

*   Exploits: Adventuresome achievements.
†   Heroic: Men and women who do extremely brave things, often in wartime.
‡   Code of conduct: The rules in life that a person lives by.
§   Patriotic: Acting out of love for one's country.

2

Doctor Hale Is Away

Date and Time: June 16, 1947—Noon

Dr. Hale pulled out of the driveway and headed towards downtown Vienna. Most of the refugee camps were off to the North and West. This afternoon, he was on his way to the Displaced Persons Hospital. David took his usual position off to the side of the castle gate and waved with his right hand, all the while gripping Thor's collar firmly with his left. Ever since Thor had his first ride in the Hale's Mercedes, he was continually anxious to jump aboard for another ride in the country.

As trained as Thor had been in the war, two years of *civilian life** seemed to have *undermined*[†]a bit his *military bearing*[‡] and discipline. This was especially evident whenever he went out to play with David only. When alone with the boy, he generally acted like other dogs unless David gave him a *command signal.*[§]

By contrast, when his real *master*[¶] Matt Hale was present,

---

* Civilian life: No longer in the Army, Thor was now a civilian.

† Undermined: Weakened or softened the strict habits he had learned in the Army.

‡ Military bearing: The serious behavior of someone in military service.

§ Command signal: A hand signal that silently told the dog to be alert or take an action.

¶ Master: A dog's master is the person to whom the dog looks for direction and guidance. Back in the Army, Thor had a trained handler who used Thor as a Patrol Dog to find enemy soldiers in battle.

Thor reverted back to Patrol Dog behavior. At those times he was neither *inclined** to be playful nor what humans might call, *carefree.†* This ability to *compartment‡* his *dual personality§* meant that Patrol Dog Thor, when the war ended, adapted smoothly to his role as the Hale family pet. After two years of tough military training and several months of harsh warfare, not all K-9s were able to make this transition to peacetime or to family life. As will be seen, even when alone with his pal David, Thor retained the alertness he had developed and shown in warfare. Thor was, after all, no ordinary family pet.

At the moment, David's mind was focused on his dad. For an instant, David's eyes and thoughts followed his father as he maneuvered the sturdy Mercedes down the long and winding road leading away from the castle. "How great it must be," David thought, "to be in Dad's shoes, fully grown up and able to come and go as one may like—no school, no homework, and no one telling him when to go to bed." Young David never considered that Dr. Matt Hale obviously had gone many years to school to become a medical doctor. He also had gone through *extensive§* military training during the war to become a senior intelligence officer—or what some people called a spy.

---

*   Inclined: To have a natural tendency towards something.
†   Carefree: Relaxed and seemingly without a worry in the world.
‡   Compartment: Maintain a distinction or separation between his role as family dog and Army K-9.
§   Dual personality: Thor is two things—a family pet and a Patrol Dog and has both personalities.
¶   Extensive: Long training lasting several months of 18 hour workdays, physical exercises, long marches with heavy backpacks, explosives and weapons exercises where they fired pistols and rifles as well as blowing up bridges and dams. There also were countless hours of classes and studying, so it was not all action stuff that the young warriors were undertaking.

Overly-simplifying* life was, of course, David's natural tendency—he saw and examined things through his eleven-year-old eyes and mind. Clearly, he could judge only things by what he had seen, had experienced or had been taught. So far, his life experience had been quite limited as well as *structured*.† Now, entering the world of spies, his life would change *decisively*.‡ To be effective in the *amorphous*§ world of *spooks*,⁋ David needed to alter his view of many things. At this point—barely ten days into spy stuff—it is fair to say that David was still very much a *neophyte*.** He still saw most things in much the same way as other eleven year olds. That would soon change.

Dr. Hale caught the image of David in his rear view mirror and he was having *parallel thoughts*††. He, however, was peering through the telescope of life from the opposite end—in his case, as a mature man thinking about his eleven year old son and about youth itself. For an instant, Matt Hale longed to be a boy again—free from the burdens of the world and able to explore the castle and Vienna with faithful Thor.

After all, life as a doctor, and then in the war as a doctor-spy, had been *jam-packed*‡‡ with demanding work that needed to be

---

*   Overly-simplifying: Thinking about complicated or unclear things in too simple a way.

†   Structured: Organized and controlled; in this case by his parents, especially his mom who had raised the children alone when Matt Hale had been off to war.

‡   Decisively: In a major or important way.

§   Amorphous: Without a fixed or firm shape or form.

⁋   Spooks: Another name for spies, who can be ghostlike in their actions.

** Neophyte: A beginner or someone who is new to an activity; in this case, to the world of spies.

†† Parallel thoughts: Thinking along the same lines such as two train tracks going along side by side.

‡‡ Jam-packed: As tightly packed as possible.

done and problems that needed to be solved. In fact, Dr. Matt Hale had not had a real vacation in seven years. "Can you imagine having a whole summer just to yourself," he wondered. He let his mind *linger** a bit, reliving in his mind the Dr. Kaminski adventure in which his son played a key role. "David performed rather well," Matt Hale thought. "Maybe he can help me again real soon—so long as his mother doesn't *get wind of it*.† She would not be too pleased if I let him get too close to any really dangerous spy stuff. But, David did show a lot of toughness. That is good; life can be tough."

Sometimes, though, even if one does not seek out danger, it comes to that person—unannounced and unanticipated. And that, precisely, was what was about to happen to David Hale. He had no idea what was coming his way—Nazi *Swastika*‡ and all.

---

*   Linger: To remain in place for a while.
†   Get wind of it/catch wind of it: Find out about something hidden, in this case David's spy work with his dad.
‡   Swastika: The spider-like symbol the Nazis used on their flags, uniforms and military equipment.

3

David Will Play

As soon as the big black sedan disappeared from view, David made a *beeline** for the kitchen. Katrina was cleaning up from breakfast and was getting ready to head down the hill to her cottage. David asked her if he could get started right away on his German language tutorial and Katrina was delighted. She immediately sensed the change in the boy's attitude which previously had been anything but positive. Katrina had no idea why David suddenly wanted to improve his German. She was pleased *nonetheless.*†

What surprised her the most was that David was eager—even smiling—as they went through vocabulary drills. To make it more interesting for him, she had him read aloud an Austrian newspaper story in German. It was about a young American who had driven his bicycle throughout the whole Russian zone of Austria without permission. Of course, being a *perfectionist,*‡ Katrina had him read the same German article ten times until he pronounced each word as well as he could. For a moment, David started wondering why he was punishing himself like this in the beginning of summer. But, he *persisted.*§

---

*   Beeline: A direct and straight course or path.
†   Nonetheless: Anyway, regardless, in any case, no matter what.
‡   Perfectionist: One who does and expects that others will do things exactly right.
§   Persisted: Kept at it and did not quit.

13

"Well, you still sound a lot like an American boy reading German," Katrina said with a stern face. "But, let's see if we can work hard enough to make you sound more like an Austrian. That would be a nice surprise for Mom and Ellie when they get back in September."

David did not react, but her comment made him think. "Hey, if I get good enough to sound like an Austrian, maybe I could be a better spy. Like Dad." That, of course, had become his own *unspoken** goal in taking the German tutorial in the first place. David asked Frau Vogel if she had a little more time and suggested she let him repeat the news article a few more times—just to see if he might get it exactly right.

The surprised woman was pleased by his request but did not show it. She had not thought he would show up for the first lesson, let alone be asking for more. They spent the next half hour working on his *pronunciation.*† When he got to the point where she seemed satisfied, he told her he would like to hold on to the newspaper for a day and surprise Dad on how he was doing.

By this time, it was Thor who was getting quite itchy—he had heard David tell Katrina that he was going exploring "outside." Once Katrina departed, the dog ran for the door with David following right behind. The bright, cloudless day was as clear as David could remember since his arrival in Austria. He told Thor to stay while he ran back into the kitchen and made his way up the back castle stairs to his bedroom. He grabbed

---

*   Unspoken: A private or secret idea that stays in a person's mind and is not mentioned.

†   Pronunciation: The way he person speaks a language and makes the correct sounds.

his binoculars and slung the strap around his neck to free his hands for his downward descent.

To make the staircase more challenging, he had begun making the plunge with eyes closed as though he was either blind or it was the *dead of night*.* In any case, it gave him a bigger thrill than doing it the ordinary way. He grinned as he imagined his mom looking on in horror should she see him taking chances that might possibly get him hurt. "Heck," he thought, "if she saw how high I go when I climb the enormous pine tree out back, she would have a *conniption*,† I am sure."

He spent the next hour with Thor running the trails that led away from the castle and down the hill towards the river. It seemed to David that no matter how hard he tried, he simply was incapable of wearing out Thor. When he occasionally stopped to rest a bit, Thor would *invariably*‡ find the nearest stick or branch to try to get the boy to run and chase him more and more.

Finally, David decided to make the woodland time more realistic. He looked at his canine pal and gave him a hand signal that stopped Thor right in his tracks. No words were used—none were required. Thor had been trained in wartime to respond to silent signals. That had been necessary whenever he was on combat patrol and German soldiers were trying to kill both him and his handler.

So, when David gave the cue, Thor stopped, perked up his ears, and waited for the next command. Thor lifted his snout,

---

* Dead of night: Late at night when everyone is asleep and things are still or quiet.
† Conniption: A sudden outburst of surprise or fear.
‡ Invariably: Always, without fail.

looked all around, and started pulling in more air which he seemed to be testing and evaluating.

This practice was deeply rooted in his Shepherd *instinct** which had been further sharpened during Patrol Dog training days. Upon arriving in France in early June 1944 to begin combat operations, Thor and his handler—an American cowboy from Montana named Mike Walker—*perfected*[†] Thor's alertness during what was some of the heaviest fighting of the war. Working as a team, Walker and Thor managed to keep each other and their fellow soldiers alive in battle after battle. Thus, when David *reverted*[‡] to using hand signals, it told this war dog that the playing around was over and his new handler, David Hale, was now in charge. At that point, the dog's character seemed to change and he was, mentally at least, back in the battle zone—fighting Nazis.

Of course, neither David nor Thor had any idea there were any real Nazis around. *Regardless,*[§] they carefully moved through the woods as though they might come across enemy soldiers at any moment. David had placed the *spyglasses*[¶] inside his carrying bag which hung from a strap over his shoulder. Together, they moved low to the ground through the *thicket.*** When they reached the *crest*[††] of a ridge or hill, they proceeded to crawl on their hands, knees and stomachs to see what lay beyond.

---

*   Instinct: The natural capabilities and habits of an animal, usually having to do with survival.

†   Perfected: To develop to the highest level of skill.

‡   Reverted: To change back to a previous way.

§   Regardless: Even though.

¶   Spyglasses: Also called binoculars, they let a person see things more clearly from a long distance.

**   Thicket: Crowded or dense bushes and grass.

††   Crest: The top.

Thor, of course, played his part and moved with the stealth of a wolf hunting a herd of caribou for dinner—even though he had eaten a full meal barely an hour earlier. After all, if David was willing to play soldier, Thor was okay playing the Patrol Dog role in these afternoon *skirmishes.** Anything was better than sitting quietly in the castle library.

Not coming upon any make-believe enemy troops by the time they reached the river, David decided to head back to the castle and climb the tower. He had no *inclination*† to stay inside on a day that felt so *refreshing.*‡ The tower would give him a fuller view of the surrounding landscape and he would be able to spot any enemy forces approaching from a distance in this mid-June *drama.*§

As boy and dog made their way homeward through the woods, several miles away two vehicles were heading in the direction of the castle. The *occupants*¶ had been there before. They, in fact, knew the castle and grounds quite well. Better even than the Hales! These were Nazi *goons*** who had lived there during the war and were secret members of the most evil organization in Germany—the *Gestapo.*†† They were not there for *sentimental*‡‡ reasons! They had been planning all this for two full years since the war was lost and they had gone into hiding.

---

* Skirmishes: A brief battle between enemy forces.
† Inclination: A feeling that one should do something.
‡ Refreshing: Wholesome and making one feel energetic.
§ Drama: A story with excitement and surprises.
¶ Occupants: People who are inside a room, house, or car or truck.
** Goons: Dangerous, brutal men who do evil things.
†† GESTAPO: The Secret State Police. The name is an abbreviation for **GE**heime **STA**ats **PO**lizei.
‡‡ Sentimental: Warm feelings that come from happy memories.

4

The Castle Parapet

As the *duo** at mid-afternoon climbed the last mound before the castle tower, David was feeling adventurous. However, he had nothing for or against which to apply his fighting spirit. No dragons to slay, no invading army to *vanquish*†, and no scientist to rescue. So, drawing on one of his favorite books and movies—*The Adventures of Robin Hood*—David pretended he was a warrior *knight*‡ and that an enemy force was encircling and preparing to attack the castle.

Staying low to the ground he reached the narrow passageway leading up to the highest point in the castle, the *parapet*.§ Thor moved with equal stealth as he had done so many times in the war. Today, he again had become the hunter—a role he played as well as any animal in the wild.

The tower had been built in the *Late Middle Ages*¶ for defense of the castle. Its high protected area enabled those defending the castle to fire arrows down on any attacking enemy. To get outside, the boy climbed through a narrow window onto the

---

*   Duo: Two of them, as in a team.
†   Vanquish: To conquer or beat in battle.
‡   Knight: A warrior who fought bravely in battle and was honored by a king with knighthood.
§   Parapet: The highest defensive place in a castle and important in defending against attack. Often a wall behind which defenders can be protected from arrows or other weapons fired from below.
¶   Late Middle Ages: The years between 1300 and 1500.

sloping roof. He then worked his way upward to the parapet itself which crowned the tower and made it a genuine *fortress*.* Thor followed right behind. This tower high point gave any defending warrior a complete view of the surrounding countryside. He would therefore have an enormous advantage over an invading force—in ancient times or even now.

The sky was clear and the sun was still relatively high in the sky. David could see several miles in all directions. On one side, to his south, David's eyes fell upon the small stream that led down the valley and connected with the mighty Danube River, eight miles away.

David felt this waterway gave him a path to all the kingdoms of the world because the Danube River flowed directly into the Black Sea. That sea in turn meant he could reach the Atlantic and eventually all seven oceans as well as the other six continents. Faraway China could be within reach so, in some ways, he could be another Marco Polo—he just needed to be a little older, have a better boat, and pack plenty of supplies to begin his global trek.

Using his spyglasses, he looked over the woods and fields leading up to the castle. He imagined he was on *guard duty*† and was searching for the invading force, one that was probably coming his way on horseback. He was glad he had worked to overcome an earlier fear he had of high places, something he had accomplished on his own in two steps.

First, when no one was watching, he climbed the highest

---

*   Fortress: A heavily protected building, castle or fort.

†   Guard duty: The time a soldier is protecting a camp or fort from attack.

tree in the woods nearby, up behind the castle. He spent a few hours swinging from branch to branch. This was followed by his second and final test—he had climbed alone up to the parapet where he sat on the castle wall and let his legs and body hang over the side. He sat and ate a candy bar and let the sense of fear he had just disappear.

At that point, he was about 90 feet above the ground, high enough to kill him if he slipped and fell. What helped him in the end was realizing that, once he got higher than thirty feet above the rocky ground below, gravity itself presented no greater danger to him than it would at either 200 or 300 feet. A fall from any of these heights would probably be deadly. Reading in his dad's medical book had helped him decide he had to do something about what Dad told him was a bit of *acrophobia*.* Dr. Hale said most people when they are young fear heights—and with good reason.

Reading always seemed to help the boy figure out the world as well as himself. One afternoon, David read an article in the *National Geographic* magazine. It showed Mohawk Indians working to build *skyscrapers*† over sixty floors and many hundreds of feet above the ground. These *ironworkers*‡ walked and worked on the buildings skeleton or steel *girders*§—in the open air with neither nets below nor safety ropes of any kind.

David mused, as he became more accustomed to high places, that he might possibly be American Indian. After all, mom's

---

* Acrophobia: A fear of heights.
† Skyscrapers: Tall buildings usually 50 or more floors or stories high.
‡ Ironworkers: Men who build the strong steel skeletons of high structures or buildings.
§ Girders: These are the strong steel skeletons that hold buildings up.

family came from *upstate New York*.* That was the home area to tribes of the *Iroquois Nation*,† including the *daredevil*‡ Mohawks who a *decade*§ earlier helped to build the mighty Empire State Building in New York City.

As David scanned the countryside to the North, he spotted a car in the distance moving slowly along the road that led up to the castle. It came to a stop by the side of the road alongside a meadow. That was where the Vogels *grazed*§ their two cows. Coming up behind the car was a motorcycle with an attached *sidecar*,** the kind used by all armies in the war. The German motorcycle with sidecar (the BMW R75) was made by Bavarian Motor Works and was the best such machine in the war. David's heart seemed to skip a beat as he recalled seeing this particular model in *Life* magazine photos of the war in the North African desert—between the Germans and the tank armies of the British and the Americans.

He squinted a bit to get a better view. He could not tell much from the distance of over a mile, but the motorcycle was clearly yellow. That was the color of the military vehicles used by the German Army in desert warfare. He also had read that in *Life* magazine. Few cars ever came up this road. So, David was instantly interested—especially since his mind was on the day's

---

* Upstate New York: The northern lake region of the State going up towards Canada.

† Iroquois Nation: The six tribes in upstate New York that agreed to not fight each other.

‡ Daredevil: People who do dangerous or risky things such as skydiving, climbing mountains, or working outside on skyscrapers.

§ Decade: Ten years.

§ Grazed: Letting animals eat grass in a field or meadow.

** Sidecar: A small wagon with a seat that is on the right or left side of a motorcycle.

make-believe adventure and *intrigue*,* the imaginary invading army, and defense of the castle by him, the loyal knight. That was, of course, make-believe stuff.

In David's real world, however, since working on the rescue operation in Linz, he had become somewhat suspicious of strangers. He had been wondering, for example, whether the Russians might somehow *trace*† the Polish scientist's escape back to the Hales. Less than two weeks into the spy business, David Hale was beginning to think like an intelligence officer—aware of the threats, risks and dangers that can happen to spies.

David crouched behind the parapet wall and occasionally took a peek. Two men got out of the car and one got off the motorcycle. The side car was empty. All three seemed to be looking in the direction of the castle. One seemed to be pointing directly at the tower—directly at David! Or so it seemed. They were too far away for him to know for certain.

Peering through his spyglasses, David was surprised by what happened next. The tall man pointed back at the car and seemed to be ordering one of the men to fetch something. That man in turn seemed to salute and off he walked to the trunk of the car to take out a canvas carrying case.

The next thing really caught David's attention—the man was holding in his hand a rifle and removing something from it. He placed the rifle and carrying case back in the car trunk and hurried back to the tall man, handing him what turned out to be a single lens *sniper scope*.‡ The tall man held it up to his eye for

---

*   Intrigue: Mysterious adventure often involving spies, criminals or murder.
†   Trace: To track someone.
‡   Sniper scope: A telescope that is used on a rifle to get a better look at a target.

quite some time as he scanned the whole castle. All this time, young David Hale was stooped down but occasionally looked out through a gap in the wall. He was not sure whether or not he had been seen or could be seen by these men.

For more than a half hour, David continued to do what soldiers and spies do when necessary—he kept his head down. Thor, soldiering again, stayed down as well. After a few minutes, the motorcycle driver and the tall man now seated in the side-car drove around the far side of the meadow. They were clearly taking a tour of the area. Each time they stopped, however, they could be seen looking in the direction of the castle—and nowhere else! By this time David knew these were not ordinary tourists. He wondered whether they too could be spies and was curious why they were there. Then, just as abruptly as they had appeared in David's world, they were gone. Both the car and the motorcycle drove away, one to the north and the other to the south. David could hardly wait until his dad got back from Vienna to tell him what he had observed.

When Matt Hale pulled into the driveway at *dusk*,* David was eagerly waiting. The doctor had a number of things running through his head. After all, he had a lot to get done before *crunch time*†which was this coming weekend when an international medical meeting on refugees would be taking place in Vienna. In addition to his medical reports he needed to prepare for the meeting, he also figured he may have some spying to

---

*   Dusk: Late afternoon when the sun has just gone down and night has not yet fully arrived.

†   Crunch time: An especially busy period when many important things are happening at once.

do. Such a conference would likely include a number of *hostile targets** in whom Visitor would have an interest.

David did not realize his dad had a lot on his mind. Nevertheless, the boy had something to say about the afternoon strangers who showed a special, in fact unusual, interest in the castle. That was certainly how it seemed to David as he recounted for his father what he had seen that day from the parapet *observation post.*†

"These are not ordinary people, Dad. I can tell you that for sure. They acted like a bunch of burglars or spies looking for a way to break into the castle." With a lot on his mind, Matt Hale told David he would chat more about it in the morning. Right now, his mind was on his next meeting with Visitor which seemed more urgent than three guys driving in the *outskirts*‡ of the castle grounds. After all, they could have been hunters.

David talked his father into playing a couple of hands of *cribbage*§ and then headed off to bed just as the moon came over the tree tops and shone a brilliant glow into the boy's room. "Okay, Thor, let's catch hold of Dad in the morning. He is, after all, a morning person—he always gets started well before the local roosters. Good night, Thor. Happy dreams, old boy. I'm sure things will be even more interesting tomorrow—for both of us I hope."

---

* Hostile targets: In the world of Intelligence Operations in the late 1940s, hostile targets meant individuals from the Communist world, especially Russians, and working with the Russians.

† Observation post: a high spot where one can see clearly in all directions.

‡ Outskirts: Surrounding area.

§ Cribbage: A card game where each player's score is recorded on a board with pegs in rows of holes.

Thor, exhausted from the day, was already asleep. Without realizing it, David was in fact really talking to himself.

5

A Secret *Rendezvous**

Date and Time: Tuesday, June 17, 1947—6:00AM

Bright and early, David went sliding down the stairwell and reached the kitchen just as Matt Hale was drinking his coffee. "Come on in, Son, and sit down. Now, tell me all about the strangers. I have some time before I have to leave for the day. Breakfast?" The boy said he would postpone eating, but was glad he could now tell the tale in greater detail. He really felt that he had *witnessed*† something important. David then proceeded to tell his father everything that he had seen.

"Dad, I was up in the tower parapet when these men pulled into the field where the Vogels keep their cows. Three men, one big car, and a motorcycle with a side car just like the ones I saw in *Life* magazine—you know, the ones used by the Germans in the desert war. The three men got out of their car and were looking around. One of them returned to the big car, opened the trunk and came back with telescope in hand. It looked like the kind the Germans used to attach with their Mauser rifles—as we saw at the War Museum. He was looking over the castle from top to bottom. Carefully. From many angles."

---

* Rendezvous: A mysterious meeting place.
† Witnessed: To see something happening, usually something important.

Matt Hale first listened carefully to the facts. Then he heard David's *opinion** and *speculation*† on why the boy thought these were in fact bad guys up to no good. "At times like this, David, it is important to trust your instinct and your gut. Nature has given us these *defense mechanisms*‡ for a reason—to keep us alive in this dangerous world. I will stop on the way out and tell Herr Vogel to keep his eye on things today—in case these guys show up again."

As David was engaged the day earlier in his make-believe *foray*§ around the castle grounds, Dr. Matt Hale was actually this Tuesday morning back in Intelligence Operations as he stopped for an inspection at the Russian Guard shack. He was entering the Russian Sector surrounding Vienna and on his way to an *operational meeting*.¶ The stop at the guard shack this time took around 15 minutes as the Russian Guard examined his travel documents, his *International Medical Credentials*,** and the one place they searched most often and most closely—the trunk of his car. Only a week earlier, that same trunk was crammed with potatoes—and an escaping Polish scientist who was being hunted by the Russian Secret Police. Today, Matt Hale had filled the trunk with medical supplies for testing and treating

---

*   Opinion: What a person thinks about a subject, a person or an event and that may be different from someone else's viewpoint.

†   Speculation: This is what a person guesses has taken place or will occur. It is also an opinion.

‡   Defense mechanisms: Nature's way of letting a person know, sense and feel when situations or people may be dangerous. It alerts a person and animals in general to danger.

§   Foray: A sudden attack into enemy territory.

¶   Operational meeting: A secret meeting between spies.

**   International Medical Credentials: Papers with his photo, name and identification as a medical doctor with permission to travel throughout all of Austria for treatment of Displaced Persons, or refugees.

refugees at a camp that had an outbreak of yet another deadly disease—*cholera.**

His trip was taking him in a northwesterly direction towards the Displaced Person Camp in Linz—the city where he and David had concluded their successful *escapade*† only the week before. On the way to Linz, he planned to stop by the U.S. Army Airbase at Tulln—some 21 miles outside Vienna but still within the Russian Sector. He had agreed to meet there with the Midnight Visitor who had sent him a message saying he wanted to discuss a few matters of importance—to Matt Hale this meant more spy stuff.

Driving in the direction of the American Airbase, Matt Hale watched for signs he possibly was being *tailed*‡ by the Russians. If he found that he was under *active surveillance,*§ he would by-pass the air base altogether and continue on his way to Linz. Later on, once he crossed the Nibelungen Bridge into the American Sector, he and Visitor could then meet *securely*⁋ at a different U.S. Army Base.

This morning, as things developed, the Russian Secret Police had their hands full dealing with food riots that had begun breaking out in May throughout the Russian Sector of

---

*   Cholera: A deadly disease where a person loses so much fluid he dies what is called *blue death*.

†   Escapade: Adventure, with some danger.

‡   Tailed: Followed by mobile surveillance, probably the Russian Military or Secret Police.

§   Active surveillance: Where the Russians would have surveillance cars and men following him all day or part of a day. *Passive surveillance* is when they would have someone in a fixed place (such as a guard post) who reports that foreigners have traveled their way.

⁋   Securely: Safely, without anyone else seeing or knowing they were meeting or working together.

Austria. Russia had been taking Austrian-grown food back to Moscow and leaving the Austrians without enough to eat.

With no sign of any Russian surveillance cars in front or behind him, and confident he was not being followed, Matt Hale drove into the Tulln Airbase. He pulled his Mercedes into one of the empty aircraft hangars. The big hangar doors closed behind him. Visitor was waiting for him. The two men exchanged greetings and went to a small conference room where they could be alone and speak privately.

Visitor began by expressing once again his appreciation for Matt Hale's assistance in last week's rescue operation. He relayed to Matt Hale that everything had worked out well in getting Dr. Kaminski to safety outside Austria. "Most of the operational success, of course, was from your *exceptional** ability to move freely around the Russian Sector— so much better than we American Military or Embassy officials are able to do. Maybe, Matt, we can make more and better use of your special *mobility*†—if you are willing, I have an idea that may help us."

"Matt, I don't need to emphasize that what you have done is really important—Dr. Kaminski already has provided us with *considerable*‡ information on the political and security *situation*§ in Poland. The Russians have been tightening their grip on the country. It turns out that Dr. Kaminski has a close childhood

---

*   Exceptional: Very special and unusually good.
†   Mobility: Ability to move around from one place to another.
‡   Considerable: Quite a bit.
§   Situation: What is going on in a place; in this case, Poland. *Security situation* would include what the Secret Police are doing to destroy freedom in the country.

friend in the Polish Government—this is the same fellow who privately warned him months back to get out of Poland because the Russian Secret Police were in fact *closing in** on him."

Visitor continued, "Kaminski believes this friend *deep down*[†] is a patriotic Pole and might even be *recruitable*[‡]—may even be willing to spy for us. His friend, according to Dr. Kaminski, is disgusted by the way the Russians have taken over all important *internal security*[§] responsibilities. It reminds him more and more of the wartime Nazi *occupation*."[¶]

Visitor ceased talking for a moment and let Matt Hale think about what he had just been told. Clearly, this was important information he had shared. As a former intelligence professional, Dr. Hale knew immediately he was being told all this for an important reason. It was not because Visitor was trying to make him feel good—Visitor wanted and was looking for more help from him.

In the world of spies, the 'need to know' rule has both a positive and a negative side to it—much like car or flashlight batteries have both positive and negative *poles*** if you wish to start a car engine or light a bulb. As a negative rule, 'need to know' means you do not tell people secret things they have no good reason to know about or understand. The positive side of

---

*   Closing in: Close to arresting him.

†   Deep down: Inside his heart and mind.

‡   Recruitable: Able to be persuaded to work secretly with U.S. Intelligence as a spy.

§   Internal security: The protection of a nation from harm by its enemies.

¶   Occupation: The period of time after the Germans invaded and were in control of Poland.

**   Poles: These are the two contact points on a battery, one with a positive electrical charge and the other with a negative electrical charge.

the 'need to know' *security principle** is that people working in spy operations must be given 'all the information needed' to be able to perform a mission or operation successfully. Knowing how much—or how little—information to reveal or share separates the good from the bad intelligence officers.

Matt Hale smiled and said, "I suppose you have heard that a medical *delegation†* from Poland will be here in Vienna this weekend for meetings on infectious diseases and other refugee issues. I assume that is why you're telling me all of this."

Visitor smiled back and said he assumed Dr. Hale would be attending those meetings. Matt Hale nodded. Visitor added, "Dr. Kaminski's friend will be here with the Polish Government group. In fact, he is in charge of Security for the Polish delegation—but still under the *watchful eyes‡* of the Russian Secret Police. As you know, Matt, even the watchdogs are closely watched in the Communist world!"

"Matt, we are not asking that you personally try to *recruit§* him. Of course! Your own medical work and excellent operational cover are too important to be risked in that way. We just need to find a way to get a message to him *discreetly¶*—without anyone else and especially the Russians knowing he has been secretly contacted by us. If you can find a way that we can do

---

*   Security principle: A general rule to protect spies and governments from enemy agents and actions.
†   Delegation: A group of people from the same country attending a meeting or conference.
‡   Watchful eyes: The Russian Secret Police are always looking; they do not trust anyone.
§   Recruit: Get him to agree to spy for the Americans.
¶   Discreetly: Privately, quietly and without anyone else seeing what is happening.

this securely—without Dr. Kaminski's Polish friend knowing you had any role in it; that would be perfect."

Matt Hale said he would see what could be done. "The first meetings will take place on Friday at one of the Austrian government buildings. I do not know where the visitors from Poland will be staying, but I know it certainly will not be the Vienna Grand Hotel—far too expensive for them. I will see what I can find out and get back to you. If this fellow is *recruitable**by us, then Dr. Kaminski will have repaid us quite well for helping him escape. Sounds good—will send you a message if I learn something."

---

* Recruitable: Able to be recruited and willing to spy, in this case for the United States against the Russians.

6

A Twin Is Born

Visitor had another proposal he wished to discuss. "For start-ers, Matt, how would you like to have a twin?" The twinkle in Visitor's eye and his *sly** way of asking made it clear there was some intentional humor in what he was asking. Matt Hale sat quietly—without responding— waiting for Visitor *to show his cards.*† As a trained doctor and intelligence officer, Dr. Matt Hale understood that one often can learn more by listening than by speaking. So, he waited for Visitor to continue.

"Getting back to last week's rescue operation and your *relatively free*‡ mobility in and through the Russian Sector," Visitor began, "what if you had another Mercedes sedan, Matt? A twin of sorts. This second one would look just like the one you're driving but it would have another secret purpose altogether?"

Still not responding, Matt waited to hear more. Visitor continued, "I read in your report how in Linz you hid Dr. Kaminski in the trunk—deep inside and behind some sacks of potatoes. It worked out fine that time. But, certainly, for the long run we need a better hiding place than that. The Russians are going to start to realize that something is *fishy*§ in your transporting

---

*   Sly: Clever and playful.
†   Show his cards: Explain what is really happening—in this case, what he means by "have a twin."
‡   Relatively free: Compared to others, such as U.S. officials, he had better freedom of movement.
§   Fishy: Funny or not right.

potatoes too often through their sector—especially now with the shortage of food and with the food riots around Austria."

Matt Hale agreed, and said he had no intention of doing that precise type of rescue operation again. "How many times can I ask David to throw up on a Russian Border Guard? Heck, if we do that over and over we might start another war." Both men had a good laugh and Visitor told Dr. Hale that he wished he had seen the expression on the face of the Russian Guard when he got doused in vomit.

"Good for David," said Visitor, who smiled and closed his eyes trying to *visualize** how surprised the Russian Border Guard must have been. Visitor went on, "A combination of raw eggs and stew, if I recall correctly. Oh yes, *Wunderbar*."[†]

Visitor went back to business and brought up the twin again. "Matt, we have an exact *replica*[‡] of your 1935 Mercedes 200 W21. It looks like yours, but with a terrific additional feature that might prove helpful *down the road*,[§] so to speak. We have constructed a man-sized concealment chamber underneath the rear seats. The way into this *cavern*[¶] is through a spring-loaded *trap door*[**] in the interior back wall of the trunk—the person can just seem to disappear. When border guards examine the trunk, they will not see anything unusual or different."

---

*   Visualize: To picture mentally.
†   Wunderbar: Pronounced "Voon-der-bar" in German. It means 'wonderful' in English.
‡   Replica: A copy of something.
§   Down the road: Sometime in the future.
¶   Cavern: A space large enough to hold a man, usually underground, but in this case in the lower part of the Mercedes.
**   Trap door: A secret, hidden door that opens and closes in a way that makes discovery impossible.

Visitor continued, "You know how am I so sure? We actually ran a series of border-crossing tests at various Russian Sector checkpoints, both in Austria and up in Germany. In fact, we both entered and departed the Russian Sector several times— and not once did they show any signs of curiosity or suspicion. Of course, we are fortunate they are not using guard dogs at the borders to sniff around our cars passing their way—at least not yet. When and if they start doing that, we are ready with some special chemicals that will confuse their dogs."

Visitor said that during his nighttime visit up from the river two weeks ago, he had spotted an old *carriage house** behind the Hale castle. He wondered whether there would be room inside there for a second Mercedes.

Matt Hale explained there would be plenty of room. He added, "*Furthermore,*† that building is not visible from the front gate or the road up to the castle. I could drive my car into the carriage house, drive out a short time later in the twin and no one outside will be able to tell the difference. Of course, that is true only if the cars not only appear similar, but in fact seem *identical*‡—the same car."

Then Matt Hale became serious. "I would need to go over this new vehicle personally with a *fine tooth comb*§ to be totally certain the twin really can appear to be my own car. After

---

*   Carriage house: An old garage or barn where carriages were stored before there were automobiles.

†   Furthermore: In addition, besides.

‡   Identical: The same in all ways and looking just alike.

§   Fine tooth comb: This is a comb with such fine teeth that it is used to remove tiny bugs from children's hair, especially in the Displaced Persons camps. Here it means to examine so carefully that any tiny difference between the two Mercedes sedans can be found and corrected.

all, the Russians—both their Border Guards and surveillance teams—are quite used to mine. They have seen and inspected my automobile countless times. I am quite certain they would readily notice any difference—if there were one."

Visitor nodded and agreed with all Matt Hale had said. And he had some good news. While they were chatting this morning, a team of American *concealment technicians** were in the hangar. They were going over both cars—Dr. Hale's and the twin—to be certain the two vehicles appeared the same. This meant tires, paint, seats, antenna, door handles, and even the sound of the engine as well as the weight of each vehicle. The only difference between the cars was that one had an invisible hiding place which was built so carefully that no one looking under the car would see anything *out of line.*† "That is accurate even if they stand right behind and peer into the open trunk," he said.

"It's really quite magical," he added with a big wide grin. "Matt, we even had one of the German technicians from the Mercedes-Benz factory work on the twin's engine, clean out the trunk, and replace the tires the other day—the man didn't notice or mention a thing about anything unusual with the trunk. It was in this fellow's factory where all Mercedes W21 models were built before the war—the factory in *Stuttgart*."‡

Matt Hale took the next hour and checked out each sedan

---

*   Concealment technicians: Men in the spy business who hide things in cars, furniture, lamps, clothing, magazines and other innocent-looking things to fool the enemy.

†   Out of line: Unusual or different. in this case, the changes that were made to the twin could not be seen from behind, from underneath, or from the inside of the open trunk. Magic!

‡   Stuttgart: A major manufacturing German city.

before driving away from the Airbase in his own car. He was very satisfied and even he could not tell the difference. He smiled as he thought about how Visitor was so careful in his spy work, but also enjoyed it so much that he was unafraid to inject some humor into things.

Matt Hale thought, "Yes, at times it's difficult enough dealing with all the poor refugees who with good reason are *depressed** about their situation. After all, they had to *flee*† their own countries. Friends and family members have been killed or are missing. And, what makes the job tougher is that I have to deal with the *dour*‡ Russians who never smile or laugh at anything in life—except when they get *roaring drunk*.§ It sure is nice spending some time with Visitor whose sense of humor by contrast is so *refreshing*."¶

The doctor-spy continued northward towards Linz, satisfied by the way the meeting with Visitor had gone. Unlike his son David, though, it was not the thrill of the spy game that attracted him—Matt Hale had seen enough action in the war for two or three lifetimes. What he currently missed most in his wartime intelligence work was being able to do something to help defeat an evil nation that was trying to conquer the entire world.

"Unfortunately," he thought, "no sooner had the Nazi butchers been defeated, then from the East came the new

---

* Depressed: Deeply saddened and sorrowful.
† Flee: Run away from.
‡ Dour: Sour, harsh and often threatening.
§ Roaring drunk: Getting so drunk that they become loud and impolite.
¶ Refreshing: Makes one feel good.

barbarians,*—the Russians. This new group, the Russian Communists, are as bad as the Nazis when it comes to *suffocating†* freedom and murdering millions of innocent human beings."

Since he arrived in Vienna, Dr. Matt Hale had been feeling increasingly like a helpless *spectator.‡* He had a *front-row seat§* on what the Russian Communists were doing in Austria itself and in neighboring Czechoslovakia. He also was hearing horror stories of Russian *brutality¶* as told by refugees from all parts of Eastern Europe. But, 'knowing something' and 'doing something about it' are entirely different. And, in his heart, Matt Hale knew that we was a doer and not a dreamer—he could not just stand aside and let evil men conquer other people, take away their freedom and, in many cases, their lives.

Simply put, Matt Hale despised bullies—whether they wore a Nazi Swastika or a Communist *Hammer and Sickle*** on their uniforms—or inside their *blackened hearts.††* When it came to wearing his own U.S. Army uniform in the war, Lt. Colonel Matt Hale wore his proudly—at least when he was not

---

*   Barbarians: Wild, murderous and uncivilized tribes that make war on peaceful nations and people.

†   Suffocating: Choking off.

‡   Spectator: One who watches things happen, such as at a sporting event.

§   Front row seat: Being so close to the action that he could see all the bad things that were happening.

¶   Brutality: The vicious treatment and torture by barbarians such as the Nazis and the Communists.

**   Hammer and Sickle: The Russian Communist symbol for their Revolution—the hammer used by factory workers and the sickle used to cut grains by farm workers.

††   Blackened hearts: Without kind or decent feelings for other people. Especially the weak and the poor.

operating under cover as a spy. Now, working against Russian Communists, he again would be putting on the unseen uniform of spies—the *cloak and dagger*.* He also would have the assistance of his 'invisible assistant,' David, who looked like any other kid. But, this 'kid' would prove to be a powerful adversary against Austria's *leftover*† Nazis and against the *hoard*‡ of spies coming to Austria out of Communist Russia.

In 1947 Vienna, both of these evil forces of Nazis and Communists were at work. A handful of wartime Germany's most senior Nazis—including Adolf Hitler—were no longer in the game because they were dead. Before he could be captured by the Russians, the Fuehrer committed suicide by gunshot. That was on April 30, 1945. Ten of the most senior Nazis were hanged eighteen months later. That was on October 16, 1946, after they had been tried in an international criminal court and found guilty of *war crimes*.§ By 1947, two years after the war, the *majority*¶ of Nazi war criminals had not yet been caught. The worst of them were still in hiding and trying to escape the *hangman's noose*** by moving out of Austria and Germany to other parts of the world. But, they could not get very far without travel documents—and they needed money, plenty of it!

---

* Cloak and dagger: The two symbols for spies—the cloak to hide him and the dagger to represent a silent weapon that makes no sound.
† Leftover: Those who had not been killed in the war or run away to other countries.
‡ Hoard: A stampeding or uncivilized army of barbarians.
§ War crimes: Evil actions such as murdering women, children, sick people, and innocent prisoners.
¶ Majority: More than half.
** Hangman's noose: The rope used to hang and kill a person.

As Matt Hale drove closer to Linz, his mind was on the Russians. He had no idea that, at that same moment, the previous Nazi Gestapo residents of the castle were planning their return visit to his very home! It would not be a *social call*.* They were going there to retrieve things they badly needed for their *getaway*† to South America. Before the war, the Gestapo had chosen the Vienna castle carefully to hide things from public view. The Nazi *ruse*‡ had worked completely—outsiders paid no real attention to the castle.

---

* Social call: When a friend comes by a home in a friendly way.
† Getaway: Escape from people who are hunting for them.
‡ Ruse: Tricky maneuver to avoid capture.

7

The Castle's Secret Past

Date and Place: Early 1940's—Secret Police Headquarters, Berlin, Germany

With the takeover of Austria by the German Army in March 1938, another German organization came to Vienna—the *dreaded** Gestapo. Its chief was the *infamous*† Heinrich Himmler, one of Nazi Germany's most *despicable*‡ leaders. Over the next seven years, he personally would order the murder of millions of human beings.

The first order of business in Vienna was to recruit Austrian Nazis to work in the Gestapo in downtown Vienna. Most of the new Gestapo members had been Vienna policemen before Austria was invaded and *forcibly*§ became part of the Nazi Third Reich.

Himmler next ordered the takeover of one of Vienna's major downtown buildings—the beautiful four-story Metropole Hotel. This historic building would serve as the *principal*⁋ Gestapo-Austria headquarters during the war. From here, the

---

*   Dreaded: Feared, scary.

†   Infamous: Known to be evil and vicious. Famous for a bad reason.

‡   Despicable: Worthy of disgust and scorn, a person who has nothing good or decent about him.

§   Forcibly: Not freely but, instead, under pressure from the invading German Army.

⁋   Principal: The main or best known building.

Nazi Secret Police ran a terror campaign that in time sent tens of thousands of innocent Austrians to concentration camps either to be worked to death or murdered. From the Gestapo's own records, it is *estimated** that 50,000 Austrians were tortured in the Gestapo-Austria headquarters before being sent to their deaths.

As Himmler anticipated, the Metropole building was eventually identified to the Allies as the center for Nazi terror in the country. On March 12, 1945, it was bombed and destroyed by Allied bombers. This was late in the war when American planes were able to reach Vienna from bomber airbases in northern Italy. March 12 was an important date for Austrians— it had been on that day back in 1938 that the Germany Army invaded and forcibly made Austria a part of the Third Reich. The bombed-out Metropole Hotel was never rebuilt. After the war, however, a memorial stone was placed on the *site*† and rests there today for tourists and Austrians to see and remember. The English translation of the memorial reads as follows:

> *Here stood the House of the Gestapo. To those who believed in Austria it was hell. To many, it was the gateway to death. It sank into ruins just like the 'Thousand Year Empire.' But Austria was resurrected and with her our dead, the immortal victims.*

Gestapo Chief Himmler was *shrewd*‡ like a good chess player—he was always thinking several moves or steps ahead.

---

* Estimated: Guessed or calculated without exact proof.
† Site: A piece of land.
‡ Shrewd: Clever, and wise like a fox.

Realizing the downtown headquarters would eventually become well known, he ordered the creation of an entirely separate but 'most secret' operations post away from downtown Vienna. This secret base would be for a private terror operation that Himmler personally would direct. No one else in Berlin even knew of its existence.

He soon found precisely the two things he wanted. First, for this special operation he used only pure-blooded Germans which is all he absolutely trusted—not local Austrian Nazis such as those who worked downtown at the former Metropole Hotel. The special castle group he assembled were chosen and sent by him directly from Berlin. He selected every member of this team, including its leader.

Himmler's second *requirement** was that the building must be *isolated*.[†] His choice turned out to be the very castle that, nine years later, would become the Hale's Vienna home. Back in 1938, the castle owners and *residents*[‡] were an elderly Austrian Jewish couple that somehow just seemed to disappear. Most people believed they left the country immediately after the German invasion, as tens of thousands of Austrians had done. In a *typical*[§] Gestapo way of doing things, however, it was Himmler who had the couple secretly arrested and sent to a Nazi concentration camp. Like so many victims of the Gestapo, they were never heard from again! With the real owners out of the way, the castle was now Himmler's. He got it without

---

*   Requirement: Something that is demanded and necessary.
†   Isolated: Far away from the busy part of a city, off in the woods.
‡   Residents: The people who lived there.
§   Typical: The normal or usual way they did things.

paying a single German *Reichsmark*.*—in his mind he *only* had to murder two old people.

The *seclusion*[†] of the castle in the hilly *outskirts*[‡] of Vienna gave it the privacy the Gestapo Chief required for the special work that he wanted to go unnoticed—even by Gestapo-Vienna! The castle was to house a *deep-cover operation*[§] controlled entirely by Himmler's headquarters in Berlin. The castle's *cover story*[¶] was that it was a quiet office for studying *human evolution*** and *genealogy*.[††] It would be made to appear as if it had nothing to do with Secret Police activities of any kind. To avoid attracting outside attention, the selected cover story was purposely meant to seem *academic*,[‡‡] even boring. It worked! For seven years of the war, the operational cover of Himmler's castle operation was never *compromised*.[§§]

---

*   Reichsmark: The German money then equal to about two dollars and fifty cents.

†   Seclusion: Isolated or away from other homes or buildings.

‡   Outskirts: An area surrounding a town or city, usually a few miles from the city center and not having many buildings or houses.

§   Deep-cover operation: An activity that is so secret that it is kept entirely away from publicly known buildings or sites.

¶   Cover story: This is the false story that is told to people to protect security and, in this case, to lead people to believe that nothing evil was taking place at the castle during the war.

**   Human evolution: How man may have developed from other animals. The Nazis believed the Germans—who descended from the Aryan tribe—had reached the highest level of human development and had a right to conquer and destroy other non-Aryan people who were inferior or not as heroic as them.

††   Genealogy: The study of family history in terms of a person's parents, grandparents, great grandparents etc. which for the Nazis was a way to learn whether a person was a pure Aryan German or may even have forbidden Jewish blood in their family history.

‡‡   Academic: Related to education and learning.

§§   Compromised: Revealed or found out.

Heinrich Himmler's brilliant criminal mind and *ruthless**
ways in time enabled him to become head of all Police and
Security organizations in Nazi Germany—beating out highly
important Nazis competing against him for power. By the middle of the war, he had become the second most powerful Nazi
in all of the Third Reich—right behind Adolf Hitler himself.
As head of both the German State Police—the infamous SS—
as well as the Gestapo, Heinrich Himmler was personally feared
as was no other Nazi. He also ran all the concentration or death
camps and was in charge of murdering the Jews and other
groups who were considered enemies of Hitler, the Third Reich
and Himmler himself.

Besides having high intelligence, Himmler paid attention to
details. Under his direct orders, the windows were covered in
order to keep secret the evil activities at the castle that included
torture and murder. Late in the war, the dark curtains prevented
Allied pilots from spotting any castle lights as they flew night-
time bombing *raids†* over Vienna. Had the Allies known what
was going on within this center of death, they would surely
have bombed the castle to *smithereens.‡* But, the old building
survived the war *intact§*—its *brutal¶* secrets remained entirely
undiscovered.

The only people in the war years to *emerge*** alive from
the castle were the Nazi killers—the small group of Gestapo

---

* Ruthless: Cruel and without mercy.
† Raids: Bombing attacks in which large numbers of airplanes dropped
   bombs.
‡ Smithereens: Small or tiny pieces.
§ Intact: In one piece, with no damage.
¶ Brutal: Cruel, wicked, violent.
** Emerge: Come out of.

officers pretending to be academic *researchers*.* Their *victims*†
were brought out always at night for burial or were thrown in
the surrounding rivers. Whether or not they had opposed the
Nazis or had been arrested by mistake, if they had even set foot
one time inside the castle they were murdered. Once they were
caught in the web of this Gestapo group, the result was certain
and the outcome the same—death! Every time. Every one.

Even two years after the war, there were no signs the Gestapo
had been there. It was David who had found some simple
German military materials both in the basement tunnels and in
the upper chambers of the castle. It was regular Army stuff the
Gestapo had left behind in their haste during their departure
from Vienna. Their flight from capture took place just before
Russia's Red Army began its *assault*‡ on the Austrian capital
city—the 2nd of April, 1945. Within two weeks of heavy fighting,
the Russian Army captured the capital city. But just a few miles
from downtown Vienna, the castle sat empty. The Gestapo had
in fact made a clean escape—well, except for one thing.

In their rush to leave, they made a mistake—they left a trail
that Thor and young David Hale would eventually follow to the
secret cache that rested in one of the castle's distant tunnels.
With all the *precision*§ that the Gestapo was so famous for in
all their evil work, how could they have *erred*⁋ so badly? What
had gone wrong?

---

*   Researchers: Men who study science and other subjects and write
    studies.
†   Victims: The people who were tortured and murdered.
‡   Assault: The attack.
§   Precision: Exactness, the habit of doing things correctly without er-
    rors or mistakes.
⁋   Erred: From the word error – they made a mistake.

1883–1938 Metropol Hotel Vienna, which became Gestapo Austria headquarters from 1938 until destroyed by Allied bombing during the war.

8

As the War Ended in Europe

Date and Place: Spring, 1945
The Place: Gestapo Castle, Vienna

In March 1945, as the Russian Red Army approached the Austrian capital, the senior Gestapo Officer at the castle received a most secret two-part message from Berlin. The first part of the *coded** message to SS Colonel Kurt Schmidt explained that a truck would arrive at the castle that very night from Berlin with an important shipment. The message directed that ALL OTHER SECRET MATERIAL BE IMMEDIATELY BURNED so that nothing remaining would show that the Gestapo had ever been there.

The second part of the message from Gestapo headquarters was truly *sinister†*—even for Nazis known for doing horrible things. It came from Gestapo Chief Himmler himself and was addressed personally to Colonel Schmidt for *his eyes only*. It was *double-encoded‡* and, because Schmidt alone had the

---

* Coded: Written in a secret code or form that other people cannot understand until the message is decoded. For example, using numbers instead of letters so that the message looks like a bunch of numbers and nothing more.

† Sinister: Suggesting a most evil action.

‡ Double-encoded: Means that the message is written in a code and then the message is encoded a second time so that the first code breaker cannot read the final message.

second code book, only he could decode it. It was brief and *to the point.**

"Colonel Schmidt: First, you will hide the shipment from Berlin in one of the castle *subterranean*† tunnels and seal off that tunnel so no one else can find it. Second, you will *execute*‡ anyone under your Gestapo command who helps hide the shipment and who you believe is not "100 percent loyal to you." Third, you will meet me on my way southward out of Germany. I will meet you at '*The Spa'*§ near Salzburg. We will return to the castle at a later date to retrieve the shipment and make our final voyage together. Heil Hitler."

It was no simple coincidence that Schmidt had been stationed at the castle. His distant cousin—SS and Gestapo Chief Heinrich Himmler—sent him to Vienna early in the war for two reasons. First, Himmler wanted to make certain that cousin Kurt was not sent to fight against the Russians on the bloody *Eastern Front.*¶ It was on that battle front where Germany suffered its greatest losses and where some 30 million people would be killed in combat between June 1941 and May 1945.

The second reason Kurt Schmidt was in Vienna was because the Gestapo Chief wanted someone he totally trusted for his castle operation. He needed a Nazi absolutely loyal to him and

---

*   To the point: Not wasting words but directly giving directions.

†   Subterranean: Underground, in the castle cellar.

‡   Execute: Murder.

§   The Spa: A code meeting place known only to both men. They had met there before.

¶   Eastern (or Russian) Front: This was the battle line where the Russians and Germans had been fighting for four years since Germany attacked Russia in June 1941. Of the 3.4 million German soldiers killed in the War, 80% of them died on the Eastern Front. It was the most dangerous place to be fighting in all wars in human history.

to him alone—one who would keep the castle secret from the other top Nazis in both Vienna and in Berlin. Himmler's initial goal for the Vienna castle was to use it for a private program to steal valuable artworks that were not already taken by the two biggest art thieves in the Nazi regime*—Adolf Hitler and his Air Force Minister, Hermann Goering.

Hitler's intention, 'after he won the war,' had been to build a 'Fuehrer Art Museum' in his home city of Linz—dedicated, of course, to himself. Thus, as the German Army marched victoriously across Europe in the early years of the war, he had his armies collecting or stealing great paintings and other art works for his Linz museum.

Why was Hitler so interested in art? Even though he had political victories later in life, Hitler in his younger years had been an extremely frustrated and failed artist. After the First World War, he twice had applied and twice was rejected for admission to the Academy of Fine Arts in Vienna. Although he considered himself talented, the Fine Arts Academy did not. Why? Well, because all of Hitler's sketches were only of things—buildings and monuments 'that had no people in them'—the Fine Art Academy suggested to Hitler that he forget trying to be an artist and instead study to be an *architect*.†

Hitler's fellow grand art thief, *Reichsmarschall*‡ Hermann Goering, loved both power and great wealth—including stolen paintings. A heroic German fighter pilot in the First World War,

---

* Regime: A particular government, and usually unlawful or undemocratic.
† Architect: A person who designs building, bridges, and monuments.
‡ Reichsmarschall: The highest rank in the German Army—above all of the other Generals.

he was famous throughout all of Germany—at times more popular than Hitler himself. As head of the German Air Force, he was given enormous powers by Hitler. Thus, Goering was able to control Nazi art theft which totaled hundreds of thousands of valuable works of art found in conquered territories. His orders to the German Army were simple—they were to divide stolen art equally between Hitler and himself.

That *fifty-fifty split** meant, of course, that there would be nothing left for other top Nazis such as Heinrich Himmler. So, the Gestapo Chief decided he would have to do something about it. And he did—he set up his own personal art theft program and based it at the Vienna castle.

By early 1945, though, it was clear Nazi Germany would soon lose the war. The Gestapo Chief by then realized—a little late to do him any good—that he needed a backup escape plan. At his Berlin headquarters, Himmler made certain that the shipment to the Vienna castle was assembled with great care. He included *forged*[†] travel documents such as passports and birth certificates as well as *counterfeit*[‡] British money. He added four bricks of pure gold, each weighing 25 pounds. The gold, of course, was stolen—it came from melted-down jewelry taken from Jewish prisoners murdered in concentration camps under Himmler's command. Himmler had been hiding it away for months, because he knew things were going badly for Germany in the war.

---

*   Fifty-fifty split: One for you and one for me, one for you and one for me.

†   Forged: Fake or falsified papers such as birth certificates, passports, and drivers licenses.

‡   Counterfeit: Completely fake money so well made that it will fool most people into accepting it as real.

The Gestapo Chief added two sets of Swiss *identity documents**—a set for himself and a set for cousin Kurt. These were in false names. Himmler, the man who ordered the murder of millions of innocent men, women and children turned out not to be so brave after all. Instead, as the Nazi empire was falling apart, he was busily putting together an emergency plan and personal *escape route*† in case they were needed. Clearly, Heinrich Himmler was not inclined to fight to the death for the Nazi cause, as Hitler had ordered his soldiers to do.

Cleverly evil and *calculating*† as he was in so many ways, Himmler completely misjudged his own situation with regard to his Western enemies—the British and the Americans. As a result of this *miscalculation,*§ he wasted several weeks trying to make a deal to surrender to the British and avoid punishment for his war crimes. In March 1945, when it was already too late for him to get away safely, he received word that British Prime Minister Winston Churchill had turned him down entirely. The British leader responded through an *intermediary*¶ that Hitler and Himmler—if they survived the war—were going to be tried and hanged for *crimes against humanity.***

How was it that this Nazi *true-believer*†† did not fight to his

---

* Identity documents: Papers such as driver's license, passport, birth certificate, credit cards and school records that are used to prove a person is who he claims to be. In spy operations, they are always fake.
† Escape Route: A path or way to avoid capture.
‡ Calculating: Carefully analyzing or thinking about a situation step by step.
§ Miscalculation: The wrong conclusion, decision or judgment.
¶ Intermediary: A person who serves as a messenger between two people.
** Crimes Against Humanity: These are quite different from the usual fighting of soldiers in war. These are murders of innocent people who are not soldiers and include women and children.
†† True-believer: One who is completely, and crazily, committed to a radical cause.

death like some legendary and heroic Germanic warrior—
instead, sneaking away from Hitler himself and the Third
Reich? It so happened that Heinrich Himmler—a chicken
farmer before joining the Nazi Party in 1927—was in some
ways a practical man. After all, raising chickens is the business
for a practical *realist** and not a dreamy *idealist.*[†]

Knowing by late 1944 that he was fast running out of time
and options, Himmler tried to give himself flexibility and a
position of power[‡] to deal with other Nazi war criminals also
on the run.[§] In his secret cache, therefore, he included travel
documents for other leading Nazis trying to escape capture. In
the shipment, he included travel papers for one hundred of the
most *notorious*[¶] German Nazi leaders—including Lt. Colonel
*Adolf Eichmann*** who organized all of the railroad shipments
of Jews to concentration death camps, and to Nazi Party head
Martin Bormann,[††] who was Hitler's private assistant for most
of the war and had been no friend to Himmler.

Many members of the SS and the Gestapo were included
in the collection. These identity and travel documents—some

---

*   Realist: A person who deals with the world as it is—that is, he is not a
    dreamer.
†   Idealist: A person who creates an imaginary world or reality in his
    mind, making him not practical in many ways.
‡   Position of power: Having the strongest position in a group, in his
    case among the other leading Nazis.
§   On the run: A person who is trying to avoid being captured by going
    to another town or country.
¶   Notorious: Most famous and most evil of men.
** Adolf Eichmann: This Nazi did escape after the war and was even-
    tually captured by an Israeli Intelligence team in Argentina, brought
    secretly back to Israel for trial, and hanged.
†† Martin Bormann: For many years he too was believed to have escaped
    from Germany but is now believed to have been killed by Russian sol-
    diers as he tried to get away from Berlin.

Swiss and most from Argentina, Paraguay, Bolivia, Chile and Brazil in South America—were the *equivalent** of a *Who's Who*[†] of Nazi war criminals. Himmler also included some *Nansen Passports*[‡] that were created back in the 1920s for refugees driven out of their homelands as a result of war. They were not by any means supposed to be issued to war criminals—ever!

Why did Himmler, at such a *perilous*[§] time near war's end, go to such trouble to pull all these documents together—even for men who opposed him during much of the Nazi period? Well, you cannot raise chickens as Himmler had done unless you are willing to do some of the detailed tasks of feeding and managing a flock of birds—animals that have small brains and few natural *survival skills.*[¶] Although Himmler was never a successful chicken farmer, he was an expert when it came to surviving in the brutal world of Nazi politics and war. During the dozen years of the Third Reich, Heinrich Himmler showed himself to be the ultimate survivor. For him, the Vienna castle was meant to play a crucial role. Right then, as Germany crumbled, Himmler needed help wherever he could get it—at that moment, the shipment sent from Berlin to the castle was it.

It made little difference to Himmler at this perilous time that Hitler's personal secretary, Martin Bormann, had long been his main enemy within the Nazi leadership. With the war almost

---

*   Equivalent: The same as or equal to.

†   Who's Who: Books that list important people in a country.

‡   Nansen Passports: After World War I, this travel pass allowed 450,000 refugees from Russia and Armenia to look for a place to live and work after losing citizenship due to the Communist Revolution.

§   Perilous: Extremely dangerous or hazardous.

¶   Survival skills: Being able to protect themselves from danger or dangerous enemies.

lost, the Gestapo Chief would have made a deal with the Devil himself in order to escape being captured by Germany's worst enemies from the East—the Russians. The massive Red Army was right then close to capturing Vienna before moving on to capture the German capital, Berlin. Like most Nazi leaders, Himmler was far more frightened of facing Russian Communist brutality than the American-British *systems of justice.**

Yet, despite all of Himmler's shrewd planning, sometimes a man's luck just runs out. After Adolf Hitler's suicide in Berlin in April of 1945, Himmler decided to make his escape. He drove in Germany southward towards *Bavaria,†* hoping to get to Salzburg in Austria to meet up with cousin Kurt. But, this once-powerful Gestapo and SS Chief never made it out of Germany.

Dressed in the disguise and uniform of a simple German Army soldier, Himmler was captured by alert British soldiers in Bremervorde in May 1945. What caught their attention were his false identity documents. Here is where Himmler's escape story becomes amusing. It was not that there was anything *technically‡* wrong with his travel documents. Ironically, his travel papers just looked 'too bloody good' as far as the British soldiers were concerned. They looked perfect—and this time, Himmler's perfectionism *did him in.§*

So, as it went, Heinrich Himmler never did *hook up§* with

---

*   Systems of Justice: The courts, legal rules, judges and lawyers who are supposed to give citizens or prisoners fair and honest trials.

†   Bavaria: The beautiful mountainous section of Southern Germany that borders Austria and Switzerland.

‡   Technically: In the details of the documents: the kind of paper, ink, printing, signatures.

§   Did him in: Was responsible for getting him caught.

¶   Hook up: Meet or connect with.

cousin Kurt. Although not nearly as clever as his evil Gestapo Chief relative, SS Colonel Schmidt was just as vicious. After all, Gestapo Chief Himmler, the butcher who ordered millions of murders without hesitation, used to *feel faint*[*] at the sight of blood.

On the other hand, Cousin Kurt, was not at all *squeamish*.[†] He had already murdered many times to keep the castle secrets and, in fact, personally enjoyed killing people! When his famous cousin was alive and in charge of the Gestapo, Schmidt *indirectly*[‡] had more power than other SS Colonels in Nazi Germany. He used that power to keep other Nazis in line as well as making them quite fearful of him. Those who knew him were very afraid to get on his bad side—otherwise, they would find themselves on the way to the Russian Front to an almost certain death.

Once captured by the British, Gestapo Chief Heinrich Himmler knew he would soon be correctly identified for the monster that he was. So, on May 23, 1945, before he could be tried and hanged for war crimes, he committed suicide. He did this by biting into a glass *capsule*[§] which released *cyanide poison.*[ꟼ] He died violently in ten minutes, but not so terribly as did millions of his wartime victims.

His art-thief *competitor*,[**] Hermann Goering, would later be captured, tried for war crimes, and sentenced to death by the

---

[*] Feel faint: When a person's head gets woozy and they begin to lose consciousness or pass out.

[†] Squeamish: Easily shocked or sickened.

[‡] Indirectly: Through someone else, not on his own.

[§] Capsule: An inch long tube.

[ꟼ] Cyanide poison: A quick-acting poison that the Nazis used in their concentration camp murders. Adolf Hitler was given cyanide capsules that he first tested on his dog, who died right away, before giving it to his wife, Eva Braun, and taking it before shooting himself in the head.

[**] Competitor: One who works against or competes against another person.

International War Crimes Court at Nuremburg, Germany. But in October 1946—the day before his scheduled hanging—he too bit into a hidden cyanide capsule and died in a matter of minutes. Where had the cyanide come from? Well, the poison capsules had been developed by Himmler's own Gestapo during the war—they were part of his program to use poison gas to kill millions of prisoners. At war's end, however, it was then used by leading Nazis to die a quick but horrible death—by suicide.

In mid-1947, after two years of hiding out in Bavaria, Kurt Schmidt was now back in Vienna. He was preparing for his return to the castle to recover what he felt was his. There was, after all, everything to be gained by taking the risk to get his hands on the hidden trunks. With his Gestapo Chief cousin long dead, Kurt needed more money. The castle gold, money, and documents would help him escape to South America.

The trove also would establish for him a strong position among those *die-hard** Nazis hoping to build a new German *Fourth Reich.*[†] The hidden cache was Kurt's *ace-in-the-hole.*[‡] If he used the documents to help top Nazis escape justice, his own power and *prestige*[§] would rise as well. So, he had no intention of letting anyone or anything stand in the way of his getting hold of the trunks he personally had hidden—and for which he had already committed two murders. The gold that once

---

*   Die-hard: Those who never quit.

†   Fourth Reich: The dream of Nazis whose *Third Reich* had just been lost in the war.

‡   Ace-in-the-hole: Taken from the world of poker, a special power or advantage over other people.

§   Prestige: Good reputation and respect from others, in this case from genuine Nazi monsters.

belonged to innocent people caught in the brutal web of the Third Reich would now be his. He would just have to eliminate or get around one more *obstacle**—the American family and dog now living in the castle.

---

*   Obstacle: Something or someone in the way.

9

Trip to the Castle Cellar

The Date and Time: Wednesday—June 18, 1947
—Mid-afternoon
The Place: The Vienna Castle—North Tunnel

At this point, everyone seemed to be at, or moving in the direction of the castle—known as the Hale Castle to young American David Hale and as the Gestapo Castle to Nazi Lt. Colonel Kurt Schmidt. Dr. Matt Hale, on his return trip from Linz, was expected home by late afternoon. David decided, after his morning's German tutorial, to head for the cellar—with Thor of course—to see what he could find or dig up. It was raining pretty heavily outside, so being in the damp basement tunnels was more appealing than being outdoors.

And the Nazi Three? They were collecting shovels and *pickaxes** to dig their way into the Northern tunnel. It was there, in March 1945, that they had buried their trunks of counterfeit British money, international travel documents and the five solid-gold bars. And, oh, the two dead Nazis. They did not know whether they would be able to start the actual digging in the next few days. They had to be sure they would not be discovered while they went about the *excavation*.† Schmidt estimated

---

* Pickaxes: Heavy sharp metal tools with handles and used to crack stones and dig huge holes.
† Excavation: Digging large holes and removing all the stones and dirt.

that they would need at least six and as many as twelve hours to break through the outside wall, get inside the tunnel, carry away the valuable trove, and re-seal the tunnel so no one would know they had been there.

Schmidt was especially interested in getting in and out of there unnoticed. He wanted to depart the Vienna region—in fact, get away from Austria altogether without Allied or Austrian government officials becoming aware that his group of Nazis had come back to retrieve buried treasure. By 1947, searching for stolen artwork and valuables had become an *industry of sorts** throughout Austria—people were searching everywhere for *loot*† the Nazis buried before the Russian attack. If word got out that former Nazi SS *thugs*‡ were actively searching in Vienna itself for valuables, the roads and border crossing points would tighten and motor vehicles would be searched more aggressively.

Schmidt told his two *henchmen*§ that, once they had the valuables in hand, they all would need to disappear into thin air—like steam from a tea kettle. He added, "Superior secrecy and perfect discipline are everything. This is a military operation—one of the first in support of the Fourth Reich. We are soldiers still. We must not fail. Germany needs us."

David, meanwhile, was fully equipped for his own trip to the basement. He was wearing waterproof boots and a warm

---

*   Industry of sorts: A kind of business, in this case one where men
      made money by finding valuables stolen by the Nazis.
†   Loot: Stolen money and other goods.
‡   Thugs: Tough, cruel and dangerous men who use violence to get what
      they want.
§   Henchmen: Thugs and rough bullies who work for criminal
      organizations.

woolen sweater Katrina had knitted him for his birthday. He also carried his Army flashlight, Swiss Army Knife as well as an empty sack to haul whatever interesting stuff he might come across. Thor, naturally, was going along to the castle *underworld** just as he was. Nature already had equipped him with everything he needed—a sharp sense of smell, excellent hearing and the hunting skills of his cousin, the wolf. It also turned out that Thor could dig quite well.

Once he got to the bottom of the long cellar stairway, David decided to head this time in a new direction—northward to a part of the *subterranean†* basement he had not fully searched before. During his first trek in that area a few weeks earlier, he found there must have been an explosion of sorts some time ago. *Rubble‡* from a cave-in blocked the tunnel itself and prevented him from traveling the full length of that passageway. Every other castle tunnel eventually led to the outside—but not the North Tunnel. All medieval castles had various escape routes—that was so people could get away from an enemy force about to *overrun§* the fortification.

When David had scouted outside along the *periphery¶* of the castle, he found a blocked entranceway that he guessed once connected and met up with the North Tunnel. He later confirmed his *hunch*** by use of his compass. It showed him that the blocked tunnel in the interior and the blocked wall

---

* Underworld: The basement area of the castle. Can also mean all the evil people who commit crimes.

† Subterranean: Below ground level.

‡ Rubble: Rocks, stones, sand and dirt.

§ Overrun: An enemy force completely conquering a fort, city, or army.

¶ Periphery: The complete or entire wall surrounding the castle.

** Hunch: A guess.

*portal** on the exterior were close to the same castle wall at the Northern-most point of the castle.

As David and Thor *slogged*[†] along the new pathway, mostly in the dark, the sounds of rats broke the eerie silence. It made the boy glad he had along an impressive *canine*[‡] to send the rodents scurrying for hiding places within and under the tunnel walls. The rats, like the Nazis, considered the castle to be theirs. As a result, anything edible under the castle became breakfast, lunch and dinner to them until any food was entirely gone. And so it had begun many hundreds of meals ago when two hefty Nazis took their *final resting place*[§] in the North Tunnel—alongside the shipment from Berlin.

The last *directive*[¶] from Gestapo Chief Heinrich Himmler to cousin Kurt was quite clear—any Nazis who knew of the treasure trove BUT WERE NOT 100% LOYAL TO THE HIMMLERS were to be *disposed of.*** Two of the German SS soldiers fit that description in Kurt Schmidt's mind. He once heard them telling a joke about Fuehrer Adolf Hitler, and Gestapo Chief Himmler. That had taken place more than a year earlier when they had been drinking too much beer and telling jokes. But, Schmidt never forgot.

So, he made certain that these two brutes carried the last of the trunks from Berlin down to the North Tunnel. Once the explosive charges had been put in place to seal off the

---

*   Portal: Doorway or entry way.
†   Slogged: Moved slowly with some difficulty
‡   Canine: A member the dog genus of animals.
§   Final resting place: The place where someone is buried or left after they die.
¶   Directive: Orders to be followed carefully.
**   Disposed of: Got rid of, eliminated or murdered.

passageway, Schmidt personally shot both of the unfortunate joke-telling Nazis. He then set the *delay timer** for the explosion and got out of there as quickly as he could.

The local rodent population living in the North Tunnel was stunned when the explosion occurred. The blasts shook their *dank,†* rocky world and made the biggest noise that they had ever heard. So they retreated a couple of hundred feet and were frozen in fear for close to half a day—until something got their attention. They smelled food. Actually, they smelled dead Nazis. And so it happened that, for weeks afterwards, the North Tunnel became the scene of rodent rats feasting on dead Nazis. Some rats even moved there from other tunnels under the castle. That process continued until there was nothing left except bones, uniforms and, of course, the Berlin shipment.

The *gruesome‡* business of the murders turned out to be "the" *telltale§* mistake the Nazis made in trying to hide the secret shipment.

Two years later, as David and Thor moved along the North Tunnel close to the area blocked by the explosions, Thor suddenly became alert. It was too dark to see, but his *hackles¶* stood up. He quickly moved ahead of David just as he had done when on patrol in the war—when he smelled enemy soldiers. Thor sensed danger for which he had been trained—trained to get out in front to protect his master. Dog and boy soon found

---

*   Delay timer: This is a clocklike device that gives the person time to get far away before the explosion happens.

†   Dank: Cold, wet, uncomfortable.

‡   Gruesome: Terrible, evil, disgusting.

§   Telltale: Something that gives away a secret.

¶   Hackles: Hair on the top of his neck that are raised when a dog gets nervous or frightened.

themselves facing the huge pile of material that blocked any further progress. David's immediate conclusion was to stop and go back. Thor, on the other hand, had something else in mind—he started digging. And dig he did!

For some minutes, David just stood there shining his flashlight on the mound of stones and dirt that Thor was attacking. Whatever it was that got the dog's attention, he intended to get to it. Seeing the determination being shown by Thor, the boy decided to help. He was soon on his hands and knees digging away. He placed both shining flashlights on a large rock and aimed them in the direction of their work site. This now had become a team effort and in this instance the Patrol Dog was leading the team. David was better able to roll away large stones—Thor excelled when it came to dealing with the dirt.

For well over an hour, they dug and pushed and rolled this material or that. David stopped from time to time to get a closer look with his trusty flashlight. They were *progressing** just fine. He concluded they would eventually make a *breakthrough*† to the other side—the tunnel ahead and whatever was over there. David had no idea what to expect—Thor seemed to have a pretty good idea! Well, at least what he could tell from his keenest sense—his sense of smell.

By this time it was getting a bit late as far as David was concerned. He was hungry and thirsty—he was dirty and tired. He reflected a bit on the world of miners and was grateful he did not have to grow up to be a coal miner. Just as quickly, he

---

*   Progressing: Getting the job done and moving forward.
†   Breakthrough: Getting past an obstacle, in this case the pile of rocks and stones blocking their way.

thought it would not be so bad mining for gold or precious stones, such as rubies and diamonds. But so far, all he had seen was worthless stuff—rocks and dirt of no value whatsoever. Not even any war souvenirs! He would have given anything to get his hands on a *German Luger*,* the really neat pistol he had seen in so many war and mystery movies before he left the States for Austria. Right then, however, his stomach growled for food. If he had a choice between a Luger and a cheeseburger, he would no doubt have asked for salt, ketchup and certainly for a burger.

The boy started putting away his backup flashlight and getting ready to quit for the day when he heard a new sound— rocks and stones went crashing downward on the other side of the wall of material. They had in fact broken through. Or better, Thor had. David crawled as high as he could onto the pile and held his flashlight up close to the stone ceiling. He could not tell for sure, but he got the feeling that they could actually get to the other side if he pushed really hard on the remaining blocking material. He figured he at least might as well see if he could create a hole to get a look.

At the highest point on the pile he started to push—little by little he could feel and hear rocks falling on the other side. This went on for maybe fifteen minutes by which time he had made a small clear opening about the size of a basketball. He then took his prize Army flashlight and peered into the darkness of what initially seemed to be an *abyss*.† Gradually, however,

---

* German Luger: An automatic pistol used by the German Army in both World War I and II as well as the Swiss and other armies throughout the world because of its accuracy and reliability.

† Abyss: A bottomless pit or hole in the earth.

as his eyes got used to the dim light in the tunnel beyond, he could see some things that looked familiar—shapes that made sense to him.

He saw three trunks seemingly no different than the regular German Army foot lockers he had found in other parts of the castle basement. And, no more than six feet away, he saw what shocked him as nothing else had ever done—he saw two German Army uniforms that seemed to be draped around a pair of skeletons. One was resting on a chair. The other was on the floor in a corner. Each one looked like something out of a horror movie.

"Oh, 'that' is what got your attention, old boy," he whispered to Thor. "Now I understand." Why he was whispering surprised even himself. He thought it just seemed appropriate under the circumstances of two dead people down there in the dark!

The skeletons alone did not shock David as they might have startled other boys his age—or even adults. His dad had a skeleton he used in the medical classes he taught before taking the Austria *assignment*.* David had gotten to the point where he could name close to a hundred and fifty human bones with little difficulty. He used to compete with Ellie to see which of them knew the most bones by name and by sight. Sister, of course, was a few thousand miles away vacationing in the *serene*† lake region of Upstate New York. At that moment, David would not have changed places with her for anything—dead Germans and all. If this was what spying is about, he was all for it!

---

*   Assignment: A job that would send him to another country to work, in this case Austria.
†   Serene: Quiet and peaceful.

But what made the skeletons weird was finding them down here in the pitch black darkness of a sealed-off *tomb**—as though they had been murdered. "What a place to die," he thought. "What a way to have your life come to an end. Scary!"

At this point two strong emotions were raging in David's body. He was still hungry, thirsty and dirty as—well—a sewer rat. At the same time, he was exploding with curiosity to get a look inside the trunks neatly stacked along one of the walls, but covered with rocks and dust from the 1945 explosion. Several questions raced through his mind.

Did the trunks hold only a bunch of Army junk? Were they empty or full? Why were the two soldiers murdered and left there before the explosion? Why was the tunnel blocked in the first place? Question after question came flashing through his mind. Each question *bred*† more questions—none of which could be answered so long as he stayed on his side of the pile of rubble and the trunks remained on the other.

"Maybe I should just wait for Dad to get home," he thought. "Or, instead, run down the hill and get Herr Vogel. But, no, Dad must be told first and he is due back home in a few hours. I'll tell him then. But, maybe I should just take a quick peek. Then, at least, I can present him with a full report—and not only a confusing mystery."

As things went, David would not be first in getting a close look at what little remained of the dead Germans, at the trunks, or the burial tomb in the North Tunnel. As the boy was starting up the pile again, flashlight in hand and getting ready to crawl

---

* Tomb: A burial place such as one would find in a cemetery.
† Bred: Created or made.

headfirst towards the other side, he felt himself being dragged backwards. The next thing he knew he was being yanked down the rubble pile to where he began. Thor, it turned out, had grabbed him by the seat of his pants and resumed his role as excavation team leader.

David was just picking himself off the ground when Thor shot up the pile and headed into the opening to the other side. All David could do was crawl back up to the top and shine his light into the chamber. Thor was all business and busily sniffing around—quite alert and looking like a dog at war.

With Thor clearly taking charge, the boy crawled through the opening and joined his buddy on the other side. And, with his sense of humor still *intact*,* David looked at the two uni-formed skeletons and murmured to Thor, "Now that there are four of us, Old Boy, maybe we can play some cards. Bridge or poker?" At that point, the only one chuckling in the cold damp death chamber was David Hale—he thought his own joke was as funny as any he had heard at the movies. Thor looked as though he had heard it all before.

---

* Intact: Whole, complete, undamaged.

10

The Treasure Trove in Hand

David wanted more light so he scooted quickly back through the hole and got his hands on the second flashlight. Then he went back into the burial chamber yet again. The boy went quickly to the trunks that had been *security sealed** before leaving Berlin back in 1945. Back then prior to setting off *dynamite†* charges in the North Tunnel, Col. Schmidt had opened the trunks to get a look. He wanted to be certain of exactly what his cousin was asking him to protect. He looked and he liked what he saw—it was exactly what David Hale would be seeing in 1947, twenty-five months later.

With the security seals broken, all David had to do was lift the latches and open the lids. Everything was in plain view for anyone to see. One trunk was stacked to the brim with *Five Pound British Bank Notes‡*—not real, of course, but counterfeit money that had been printed under Himmler's orders at the Nazi concentration camp at Sachsenhausen, Germany. Bundled in stacks the size of a small loaf of bread, there obviously was a *king's ransom§* worth of English money—but only if it all were genuine and not fake.

---

* Security sealed: Wrapped with special materials and markings that would show whether anyone had opened the trunks.
† Dynamite: Explosive material that is used to blow up rocks to build highways or buildings.
‡ Five Pound British Bank Notes: British money came in denominations of 5, 10, 20 and 50 Pounds.
§ King's ransom: This means a huge amount of money, enough to pay to rescue a king who may have been taken prisoner by an enemy.

The huge pile of British Notes gave David a pretty good idea why the North Tunnel had been sealed off. It became clearer still when he reached into trunk number one and tried to lift a heavy object wrapped in a leather pouch—it turned out to be solid gold. It was the heaviest material he had ever tried to lift. The German Eagle design stamped into the bar made it seem like it could be the real thing. All he could say was "Wow" and then "Holy Moses." If this were really gold, David now understood why the murders had occurred.

The third trunk didn't look special to him. When he lifted the lid, all he saw was a bunch of papers and photographs. It would turn out that the third trunk was in fact the *jackpot.** More valuable than the gold or paper money? Absolutely! These were documents assembled personally by Heinrich Himmler to assist escaping senior Nazis—men who could not get far traveling with their own passports or identity papers. The top Nazi leaders of the German Third Reich were *infamous†* far and wide. At war's end, Intelligences Services, Armies of the world and victims of Nazi brutality were trying to find them—not to honor them but to hang them.

Looking once again into each of the three trunks, he saw three more leather pouches, each holding a gold brick. David weighed his next move. He certainly could not carry much of the buried loot on his first trip. He had only brought one carrying sack—it was a fairly long distance through the tunnel just to get back to the stairs. Then he would have to haul it up the extremely long stairway to Dad's study which he decided would be his first destination.

---

* Jackpot: The biggest prize of all.
† Infamous: Famous for being evil men or criminals and murderers.

He didn't waste any time *mulling things over**. He grabbed the first heavy gold bar, scooped up a bundle of the British money, and he added four packets of travel documents with photographs. All of it went into his carrying sack. He then re-covered both flashlights and said to Thor, "We're getting out of here, old fella. We're not passing 'Go' and we're not collecting two hundred dollars." Obviously, the language of his favorite board game—*Monopoly*—had come to mind in his excitement. Right now, he was dying to get the stuff and the news to his father. "Sure hope he is home pretty soon. He'll know what this is all about—if anyone does."

Ten minutes later, huffing and puffing as the dirt-covered boy opened the door to Dad's study, his *heart sank*†—all he saw was the empty desk and his father nowhere in sight. Nor was there any sign he had even arrived home. David then slid the carrying sack under the great desk and headed for the door to the yard.

He glanced down the hill to the Vogel house, hoping Dad had stopped there on the way home. No sign of him there, either. Then, with Thor in close pursuit, he headed for the parapet. If his dad were fairly close to the castle, David would spot him several miles away. As he got to the *pinnacle*‡ and searched the road from the west, he saw no sign of Matt Hale. Just as he was about to descend to ground level, he took a last westward look—a familiar car was coming in his direction. It was a Mercedes all right, but not the Hale car—it was the same Mercedes he had spotted earlier in the week. The strangers had

---

* Mulling things over: Thinking carefully and thoroughly about all the possibilities.

† Heart sank: He felt let down and disappointed.

‡ Pinnacle: Highest point, the top.

returned! This time, though, the large sedan did not stop in the field or make a turn away from the castle. It drove straight up the hill to the castle gate, pulled to a stop and a tall man got out. He looked around while the driver stayed in the car.

"Son of a gun," David muttered, "they could be here for the trunks!" Feeling suddenly a bit unsteady on his legs, he sat down against the wall and tried to calm down his heavy breathing. The next thought that entered his mind was as *logical** as it could be, "If they are in fact interested in the trunks, then these guys could be the murderers! Oh, *shucks,*†where's Dad? Have to think. What would Dad do if he were in my position?"

The boy decided that the best thing he could do is find out what was going on with the strangers. As Dad had taught him when giving the boy target lessons with his pellet gun, he first had to breathe properly if he was going to get good results in anything. So, while Schmidt stood by the closed gate and looked impatiently all around, young David Hale sat a couple of minutes with his back against the parapet wall and took in slow deep breaths—"in through the nose and out through the mouth," was what Dr. Hale taught him.

By the time he got up and headed for the stairs, the junior spy was calm—and ready for action. If David could have described how he felt at the moment, he would have said "excited, not fearful."

He was pleased with how he had recovered from his sudden fright. "Darn adrenalin," he muttered. As he descended the

---

*   Logical: Clear thinking that makes perfect sense.
†   Shucks: An exclamation or word used to express sudden disappointment or unwelcome surprise.

tower stairway to go down the hill to the front gate, he whispered to his partner Thor, "Listen, my pal! The good thing is we know some things about these strangers—they will think I am just a kid who knows next to nothing—and you are just any old dog. Let's go and see what's up. Let's try to do what Dad would do."

By the time David reached the gate, Herr Vogel was already there and speaking with the tall stranger who was chatting away in German. The Nazi paid no particular attention to the boy as he and the dog approached. He did however cast a wary glance at Thor who stayed close to David and was neither wagging his tail nor showing any obvious signs of *aggression**—or friendliness. Thor kept his eyes focused entirely on the stranger. To Schmidt, it was clear that Thor was quite alert and likely to stay that way. "This is not your average pet," he thought. And Schmidt was correct—Thor was on patrol.

Herr Vogel—who had been *forewarned*† by Matt Hale about visitors roaming around the fields—told the tall stranger that the castle was now occupied by an international medical family and that they had been there for several months. "Nice family. The father fixes sick people; lots of them" was how he put it.

Schmidt asked about the family that owned the castle and lived there before the war. He, of course, was quite aware that his cousin had sent the old man and woman to their deaths at the Mauthausen-Gusen Concentration Camp. Schmidt falsely claimed to have been an old friend of that family. He lied even further that he was hoping to see whether they had returned to

---

*   Aggression: Being unfriendly and willing to attack.
†   Forewarned: Told before or in advance.

their beautiful castle home. He went on to *claim** that he used to visit the family in the 1930s and "hoped they had survived the war okay." To make it seem true that he and the old couple were friends, Schmidt added that he had some old photographs to give them—Schmidt, obviously, had merely found them in the castle during the war.

Well, if Thor had a good nose for danger, Herr Vogel had a superior nose for Nazis—no matter how they tried to mask their *true selves*.† He had gotten through the war alive precisely because he could tell the difference between a patriotic Austrian and a secret member or *informer*‡ of the Gestapo. And, in this tall German stranger, Konrad Vogel smelled Gestapo. Schmidt's *arrogance*§ was crystal clear. So, when the tall stranger asked David why he looked like he had been working in a coal mine or river bed, Herr Vogel spoke up to protect the boy from any suspicion—"been digging potatoes for me and doing a great job—mud and all."

Vogel then told the tall stranger he did not know the family who lived there in the 1930s. He suggested that Schmidt call Dr. Hale when he gets back later today as he might have some information. He gave Schmidt the Hale telephone number at the castle. At that point, the stranger thanked Vogel, glared back at Thor, got back in the car, and left. As the tall stranger left, the hackles on Thor's back fell back into place.

---

*   Claim: To state something new that may or may not be true. In this case, it is a lie.

†   True selves: The real person, not the one he might try pretending or appear to be.

‡   Informer: A person who secretly reports to the police, usually against his own countrymen.

§   Arrogance: A bad, mean attitude of a person who thinks he is better than other people.

The strangers had no sooner gotten out of sight than Matt Hale came driving in from the opposite direction. He was surprised to find David down near the gate with Herr Vogel. He was *chagrined** to find his son looking absolutely filthy from head to toe. "What on earth have you been up to, Son? Fall in the river? Jump in the car and go take a bath before dinner. You must have a lot to tell."

Not wanting to speak freely about the North Tunnel caper in front of Herr Vogel without his father's permission, David just mumbled an "okay" and got in the car for the short ride up the hill. Thor had already reached the kitchen door when they arrived—he too was looking dirty, *famished*[†] and anxious for a meal. Matt Hale glanced at Thor and said, "You too? What a mess! You guys have been quite busy I see. I hope you have something good to show for it."

"Have a lot to tell and show you, Dad. Has been an interesting day. You may not believe what we—Thor and I—*came across*."[‡] Few things surprised Matt Hale any more—he had seen enough to fill a dozen books on medicine, war, spying and refugees. This time, however, would be different. He would be indeed surprised when he learned what David had been up to—and particularly by what he had found.

---

*   Chagrined: Completely surprised, in fact stunned.
†   Famished: Deeply hungry as though he had no eaten in a long time.
‡   Came across: To find by accident.

11

Baiting the Trap

The Date and Time: June 18, 1947—Early Evening into Night

Dr. Matt Hale had returned from seeing Visitor and visiting the Linz refugee camp with the firm intention of using this evening to prepare for a quick trip into downtown Vienna in the morning. He had to *case** the meeting site of the international medical conference. He was a bit *pressed for time*[†] because the Polish Security Official whom Visitor wanted to meet—Dr. Kaminski's friend—would be in Vienna for only four or five days—six at the most. "Not a lot of time to contact, get to know and recruit someone," Matt Hale was thinking—"and then train him in *tradecraft*[‡]—if he says Yes."

Matt Hale was *intimately*[§] familiar with recruiting and had accomplished it in far less time—under far more dangerous conditions—in war time. In one case, he recruited a leading German rocket scientist at a *resort spa*[ꟗ] near Salzburg that was used by Third Reich leaders and their families. In that operation—in disguise, using an *alias*** and playing the role of a Swiss

---

*   Case: Check out or have a good look at.
†   Pressed for time: In a hurry.
‡   Tradecraft: The secret tricks and ways a spy carries out his work and keeps from getting caught.
§   Intimately: Closely and deeply.
ꟗ   Resort spa: A vacation area with warm water springs where people rest and often recover from illness or to get back in good shape physically.
** Alias: False name.

wartime banker—Lt. Col. Hale made his *recruitment pitch.**
He knew he would be hanged as a spy if the rocket scientist,
rather than saying "Yes," had instead called in the Gestapo.
That scientist did say "Yes" and, in turn, soon played a major
role recruiting other German rocket engineers to go with him
to the United States after the war.

The Americans first helped scientists avoid being kidnapped
by the Russians. Dr. Hale's medical skills came in handy also
in helping this scientist stay in Salzburg several weeks to avoid
returning to his job—his German rocket center was scheduled
in the following weeks for massive bombing by the British and
the Americans. So, there was a pretty good chance the scientist
would be killed if he went back to work.

How could this healthy young German scientist avoid returning to the rocket center? Hale gave him a crash course
in *malingering.†* Hale, the doctor-spy, made it seem that the
scientist was suddenly quite sick—even though he was not. To
bolster‡ the case, he gave the scientist some medications that
made it seem as though he suddenly had serious heart disease
and could not travel at all.

When it came to the business of recruiting, therefore, Matt
Hale had done it before and done it well. Furthermore, while
helping the scientist remain in Salzburg, Hale was able to
collect from him valuable information and sketches on the

---

* Recruitment pitch: That is the moment a person is asked to cooper-
ate with an intelligence service in secret operations, in other words,
spying.
† Malingering: When a healthy person pretends to be seriously sick so
he can get out of work, school, a test or travel—and succeeds in fool-
ing other people—even doctors.
‡ Bolster: Make stronger, strengthen.

leading German rocket scientists as well as the latest German rocket program—*critical** intelligence reporting that Hale sent by shortwave radio back to U.S. Army Headquarters in London and Washington. Assisting him in this operation was his wartime contact, Herr Vogel, who was with the Austrian Underground Army active in the Salzburg area at that same time.

Well, after David had taken a bath and eaten a quick dinner, father and son went into the study to talk. As he went behind his desk, Matt Hale spotted the sack David had deposited underneath. "What have we here, Son? Let's take a look." What he felt when he lifted the heavy sack got his interest. He smiled and asked if David had begun collecting rocks and boulders, or something. "Not a lot of precious jewels in this part of Austria—so it must be something else, right?"

"Better look Dad. I think even *you* could never guess."

Matt Hale emptied the contents of the sack onto the rug and got one of the shocks of his life. He recognized the Third Reich Gold Bar for what it was. He saw the packet of British money and guessed correctly that it was counterfeit. And he was familiar with two of the Nazi leaders whose photos appeared with false names on the travel documents—Adolf Eichmann and Aribert Heim—each of whom was wanted far and wide for war crimes.

Adolf Eichmann had been the Gestapo Chief in charge of transporting millions of Jews and other civilian victims of the

---

*   Critical: Highly important; in this case, of significance to the
    American military, scientific, and political leaders at the White House
    and the Pentagon.

Third Reich to death camps across Eastern Europe. Aribert Heim was the Nazi monster who conducted deadly and gruesome medical experiments at the Mauthausen death camp in Austria. A member of the Nazi SS, Dr. Heim was known in the death camps as "Doctor Death" for all the murders he committed.

Matt Hale let out a low whistle and said, "Son, what have you been doing? Tell me how you came across all this. And where—the tunnel?"

The boy explained the afternoon adventure in great detail. Over dinner, he had mentioned to his father about the two skeletons and the German Army uniforms. He now told his father that he had brought up from the North Tunnel only a small fraction of what Thor and he had discovered. "Three full trunks, Dad. FULL! Looks like there are four gold bars in all. Also, a whole trunk with nothing but money. And the third trunk? It is stuffed with papers and photographs."

Leaping ahead, the boy continued: "But Dad, I am afraid the strangers who were sneaking around here the other day—and who came by here again this afternoon—may be after the same stuff. Just guessing, but I have a funny feeling that is the case."

He told his father about the conversation Herr Vogel had with the tall stranger at the gate and explained that his dad may be getting a phone call. "The tall guy in the Mercedes said he was an old friend of the family living here before the war. He said he wants to find them. I could tell that Thor did not like him one bit."

The pieces of this complicated puzzle fell into place pretty rapidly for Matt Hale. Since the war ended, he may have mainly been doctoring—his instinct as an Intelligence Officer, however, had not disappeared. He knew some things from Visitor and from his own wartime experience that *shed light** on the three items David had carried up from the tunnel and were now resting on the rug in his study.

He could tell by its weight and *look†* that the bar was indeed gold. He knew also the background story on Sachsenhausen Concentration Camp and *Operation Bernhard‡*—the Gestapo's secret program to print counterfeit British Notes or money. At Sachsenhausen, the Nazis used Jewish prisoners—men who had been *engravers§* and in some cases *forgers¶* before the war—to do the difficult printing. These Jewish prisoners had been kept alive by the Gestapo only because the Nazis needed them to print millions of fake British Pounds. Otherwise, they would have been put to death much earlier.

That fake money, though not perfect, looked and felt much like real British Bank Notes. The original Nazi plan had been to drop millions of the bills from German airplanes all across England as a way of creating *turmoil*** in all of England—possibly breaking or ruining their *economy.††* By the time the money

---

* Shed light: Made it clear or understandable.

† Look: The way it appeared or seemed to be.

‡ Operation Bernhard: The secret German program to hurt England by printing and distributing fake English money.

§ Engravers: They make the printing plates used by governments to print money. Most engravers are honest and work for governments—others are criminals who print counterfeit money for themselves.

¶ Forgers: Skilled artists and printers who are criminals and can print money that looks real, but is not.

** Turmoil: Chaos and confusion.

†† Economy: The whole system of businesses, workers and governments that make, buy and sell things and use money to pay people for work, pay their taxes, or put extra money in banks as savings.

was all printed and ready, however, it was too late—the war was just about lost. So that Nazi plan was canceled.

Then, it so happened, Himmler found another use for the Sachsenhausen fake British Bank Notes—he began paying spies around the world with the counterfeit money. Himmler was so pleased to have the additional *funds** that he decided to keep his printing operation forever secret. To protect the secrecy of Operation Bernhard itself, he ordered that all 142 prisoners who worked on the printing operation be murdered. But, by sheer luck and *chaos†* as the war was ending, those prisoners were transferred away from the Sachsenhausen death camp. They were then *liberated‡* in Austria by soldiers of the U.S. Army. As a result, the Gestapo's secret counterfeit money operation was *exposed§* to the Allies.

After the war was over, the British and American Governments were able to find and recover much of this counterfeit money—that which had been dumped by the Nazis into Austrian lakes in waterproof containers. But, no one had caught up with the trunk of Five Pound Notes hidden in the North Tunnel of the Hale Vienna castle.

"The North Tunnel, you say, David? Let's have a look." They headed for the basement and brought along more carrying sacks—and a shovel. Thor went too and took up his patrol position as they got close to the *remains¶* of the two dead Germans. He knew they were not alive—he was being

---

*   Funds: Money.

†   Chaos: Total confusion and mess.

‡   Liberated: Freed, set free.

§   Exposed: Revealed or found out.

¶   Remains: The body and bones of a dead person.

*prudent** and, yes, making certain. For Matt Hale to get into the burial chamber, he had to widen the hole. This time, he did the digging which went pretty quickly. They also had better light because he had brought along two *paraffin*† lanterns that let off a pretty bright glow.

Once inside the chamber, it did not take long for Matt Hale to examine the three trunks. He told David to prepare for a long night. They were going to be taking some pictures—the boy would be playing an important role. They loaded the carrying sacks with the travel documents and photographs for what Matt Hale now called "The Nazi 100." They left behind the two other trunks as they were—one with the gold and the other with the British Bank Notes.

David, a bit surprised, asked, "Hey Dad, why are we not taking it all? Why just the papers and photographs?"

"Well, Son, I have a plan and right now we first have to make sure we make a record of all these photographs and travel documents—before we give them back to the Nazis who put them here." It was David's turn to be shocked—he was shaking his head as he asked, "Why in the blazes would we ever do that? Whoever did this are murderers, Dad. Nazi murderers!"

"And that is why we want them to get their loot out of here and to never come back—to the castle—to our home. I need to keep you, Ellie and Mom safe from these monsters. The best way to do that is let them think they got away with everything. We have no idea how many other Nazis these three strangers

---

*   Prudent: Using good judgment; being careful; cautiously wise.
†   Paraffin: An oil used around the world in lamps and lanterns where
     electricity is not available. In the United States and Canada it is called
     kerosene.

may have told. I have no desire to let this castle become a target of those looking for treasure and travel papers—especially
gold! But, first, we have to *bait the trap** in such a way that they
will get stuck in their own mess."

After getting the stuffed sacks of documents to the stairway
and upstairs to his study, Matt Hale suggested that David go to
the kitchen and make himself a sandwich. When the boy had
left the study, the senior spy opened his *concealment device*†
built into a closet. He pulled out the hidden radio he used to
send a coded message to "Visitor." Hale called for an emergency
meeting that night at midnight and suggested Visitor come up
from the river "in case the castle is being watched."

He had no sooner sent the secret message and received an
answer back that Visitor would be there as requested, when
the telephone rang.

Matt Hale picked up the phone and answered in German,
"Doctor Hale, Good evening." As expected, it was Schmidt who
then identified himself falsely as Manfred Becker, an old friend
of the unfortunate Glasser family who lived at the castle before
the war. Schmidt repeated his lie that he was looking for the
Glasser couple and had some photographs to give them—just
as he had told Herr Vogel in the afternoon.

At that point, David strolled into the study and his dad
put his finger over his lips so the boy would know enough
to sit down and say nothing. After a couple of minutes of
hearing Schmidt telling other meaningless lies about "his old
friends, the Glassers," Matt Hale abruptly told Schmidt he was

---

*   Bait the trap: Putting something attractive in a trap to catch the prey
     you are after.
†   Concealment device: Anything built to hold a spy's equipment or ra-
     dio; in this case, a false ceiling where the radio equipment was hidden.

busy—too busy—to chat right then and that he was preparing to leave town for a week. "Call again or come by here after the 25th of June—when we return. In fact, July would be better. In a rush. Have to go. Good bye."

At this point, with the phone call ended by Matt Hale, Schmidt was *fuming**—almost in a rage. As a former senior Gestapo officer and Nazi, he was not used to having anyone *dismiss*† him—as though Schmidt were some *low-level*‡ private in the Army. He had a *crazed*§ look in his eyes and let out a string of curses that not only shocked his two Nazi *under-lings*ⁱ—but terrified the pair.

Then, just as quickly, he let out a roaring laugh. "What am I saying? This is good news—very good news—wonderful news! While this stupid Doctor Hale is away, we will go in and get our stuff. Hale can then wait for my phone call *until Hell freezes over.*** By next week we will be in France. In the great city of crime—my kind of city—Marseille!††"

In the study back at the castle, Matt Hale was smiling as well. He looked at his totally-confused son and said, "David, there are *many ways to skin a cat,*‡‡ as the saying goes. But right now, we are about to skin some Nazi skunks—or make sure others skin them before this is all over. That will be perfect. Okay, partner, let's get photographing."

---

* Fuming: Exceedingly angry though trying not to show it.
† Dismiss: Send away, told to leave or go away.
‡ Low-level: Unimportant.
§ Crazed: The look of a crazy person or wild animal.
ⁱ Underlings: Those who were lower in rank or power.
** Until Hell freezes over: An expression that means forever and ever.
†† Marseille: Pronounced "mar-SAY," an important French city on the coast of the Mediterranean Sea.
‡‡ Many ways to skin a cat: To get something done or finished.

12

Poisoning the Well*

Matt Hale was glad that he had recently received a *considerable*[†] supply of *35 millimeter film*[‡]—photographing as many as a dozen pages for each of 'The Nazi 100' would take a lot of that film and most of the night. The good news was that the chore of *developing*[§] the film would belong to Visitor's staff back at the Embassy.

So, the father got David organized to *tackle*[¶] each packet of documents *individually*[**] and keep them from getting all mixed up. The boy would have to make a list of each Nazi's name and make sure that the documents were put back together in the same order as they were found. Once David started working with the system, he found it wasn't hard to follow. However he could not read what he was copying—it was all in German. After a while, he got a bit tense looking at the *sullen*[††] faces of some of the world's worst murderers. In a way, each had the same scary look as the tall stranger did.

---

* Poisoning the Well: Making sure that the thieves get away—not with something useful—but with a poison of sorts.
† Considerable: A large amount or supply.
‡ 35 Millimeter Film: Also called 35MM Film, the most popular Black and White photographic film in the 1940s.
§ Developing: Taking photographing film and turning it into paper photographs by use of chemicals.
¶ Tackle: Handle.
** Individually: One at a time.
†† Sullen: Lifeless, expressionless, without a good expression.

While the junior spy went about his *assignment*,* he was feeling energized—he had not slept in close to 20 hours, but he was as wide awake as he could ever be. It would never have occurred to him to take a rest or go to bed—not with all this stuff going on! His dad had said this was important—that was all he really needed to hear.

Matt Hale, meanwhile, had returned to the North Tunnel and brought up the other three leather pouches holding the remaining Third Reich Gold Bars—all seventy-five pounds of it. The fourth 25-pound bar was in the study. He wanted them on hand when Visitor showed up. As the big Swiss clock in the hall struck midnight, Matt Hale heard a tapping sound at the study door leading in from the garden. Visitor of course had arrived as scheduled, also looking as bright and wide awake as the boy in the study working the camera all evening.

Matt Hale took Visitor to the kitchen for a coffee and made a cup of hot cocoa for David to whom Visitor gave a warm greeting. He thanked the boy for all he was doing. Visitor again referred to the recent rescue operation in Linz and congratulated David for what he had helped achieve. "And now, I see, tonight you are one of the most important photographers in all of Austria. Your dad must be real proud of you. I am."

David grimaced, took the chocolate drink and headed back into the study to continue with his work. He was not, at this point, interested in standing around being praised—or losing time chatting about the past. He knew he had to keep his mind on what was going on right now. The hot drink gave him the energy boost he needed—he was glad for that.

---

*   Assignment: The task or duty he had been given.

Seated at the kitchen table, coffees in hand, Matt Hale outlined what had been found, how much there was of it, and what he thought was the best way to *turn the tables** on these Nazis—brutes who so cleverly had buried a treasure trove that would serve their purposes in other parts of the world for years to come. His proposal to Visitor was in some ways simple—in other ways quite challenging.

First, Matt proposed that they let the Nazis get away with their loot—and do nothing that would let them know the Americans were aware of what was going on. He said, "Right now, David is photographing each and every document and picture of 'The Nazi 100.' These were top leaders in the Nazi SS, the Gestapo and in the Nazi Party of Germany. I have examined the British Bank Notes and want you to *verify*† what I think is the case—that all these Five Pound Notes are Nazi counterfeits—probably came from Operation Bernhard."

Matt Hale continued, "Finally, I am sure no one would want to just give the Nazis four Third Reich Gold Bars. That would be worth a great deal of money to them. So, if it is possible, I suggest we 'poison the well' in such a way that the Nazis will do poorly with their stock of gold—gold bars just as fake as their Bank Notes. Simply put, within 24 hours, can you get me some replacement bars that are real heavy, have a gold outer layer but are solid lead on the inside? And, of course, each bar will need the Third Reich design stamped into it—exactly like the real ones I am giving you to take along. And tonight, can you haul away this 100 pounds of real gold? You sure look strong enough for that."

---

*   Turn the tables: To change things around so they are the opposite of what they were.

†   Verify: To say whether my conclusion is correct or not.

Visitor laughed and said he had never carried 100 pounds of gold before, but was sure he could make it. "Matt, is that all you will need from us?"

"Not entirely. I need to make the inside of the tunnel look more or less like it was before David and I dug our way in. So, after we *restore** the three trunks with their earlier contents, I need to make a small explosion to scatter rocks and dirt all around. Then, if the Nazis try to dig their way in from the blocked outside entrance—as I expect they will do—they will not think anyone else had been there since they blew it up. That was in early 1945 I would guess. Can you get your hands on a smallish explosive device that will do the job—but not destroy the trunks or blow the castle off its foundation?"

Visitor said he would certainly do his part—the following night he would be back at midnight with the things Matt Hale requested. "You know, Matt, lead-filled bars the same size as the solid gold bars will not weigh as much. As heavy as lead happens to be, gold is almost twice as heavy. Let's hope these Nazis cannot tell the difference. By the way, our *craftsmen†* will probably use a small part of the gold from the Third Reich bars to make our fake bars look real, just enough for a good coat-ing. The great thing about gold it is that is just about the most *malleable‡* of metals—it can be shaped and will easily coat or cover a solid chunk of lead. When we are done, they will look just like solid gold bars."

---

*   Restore: To put back in the original, initial or beginning condition.

†   Craftsmen: Men who work with their hands and are able to build things with wood, metal, cement and any other materials needed in an intelligence operation.

‡   Malleable: Able to be shaped in many different ways, even in thin layers.

Visitor then handed Matt Hale a packet of information and a photograph of the Polish Official due to arrive in Vienna for the medical conference. "I hope, Matt, you will still have some time to help us on this one, too. This darn Nazi stuff is really a *time-consuming** step backwards—into the ugly past. These days, we worry more about the Russians, frankly. But, former Nazis are a threat also—many of them will be working in the future for America's enemies around the world."

Visitor continued, "The Polish Official we need to get to is Major Otto Gorski. He was married, according to Dr. Kaminski, but his wife was killed in the war. Gorski has two children who are currently being raised by his sister who lives outside of Warsaw. According to Dr. Kaminski, Gorski would probably not return to Poland from Vienna except for his children. He said he cannot think of leaving his kids behind to grow up alone under Communism which is the way Poland is going. He got into the security field with the help of an uncle who is close to the Russian authorities. Major Gorski, however, is a Polish *nationalist†*—but these days a secret one. It was only through the help of his uncle that he too was not executed during the war by the Russians in the Katyn Forest *massacre.‡* Gorski took great personal risk in warning Dr. Kaminski that the Russian Secret Police were after him. For that reason, we think he may be happy to talk to the Americans—if it can be done securely."

Matt Hale *reassured§* Visitor that he would be quite involved

---

*   Time-consuming: A project or job that takes a great deal of time.
†   Nationalist: A person who is very loyal to his country, in this case to Poland.
‡   Massacre: The murder of a great many people.
§   Reassured: Telling him that things will be fine and that things will work out.

in that conference and be looking for Gorski. He said he was taking David to Vienna for the weekend as part of his plan to mess up the gold-hungry Nazis. "Yes, I have to leave this place empty so they come back and, well, steal back their stuff. The timing of the conference in fact is perfect for me."

As Visitor got ready to leave, he said he had better take a look at the tunnel to make sure he brings back the right amount of explosive material—maybe just one stick of dynamite or enough plastic explosive for a tiny "boom." Visitor then smiled and said, "Sorry, but the rules say the leftover* gold will have to go into the *U.S. Treasury.*† Too bad! Almost 100 pounds of gold could make you rich, Doctor Hale. Very rich. And, by the way, I have to get approval from the Intelligence Group for how we are dealing with these Nazis. But, I don't believe it will be a problem."

---

* Leftover: That which was remaining.
† U.S. Treasury: The department of the American Government that prints our money.

13

Leaving Open the Trap Door

The Date: Thursday – June 19, 1947

The first thing Matt Hale did in the morning was walk down the hill to have a brief chat with the Vogels. They discussed the Nazi strangers. Matt Hale explained the general background of what David had found, where it had been buried, and why he wanted the Nazis both to get their treasure back and leave the area for good. Herr Vogel said he would move the cows to another farm and do their own *disappearing act** by leaving town today. They would drive out to Salzburg for a few days. "If the Nazis are watching the castle, Dr. Hale, they will see us leave town."

Matt Hale grinned and said, "The only thing more we could do is put out a large sign in German saying 'Hey, Nazis: The Place is empty—Come back in and get your stuff.'"

Schmidt, meanwhile, had indeed put his two goons to work keeping track of the *comings and goings†* at the castle. He ordered that the gated entrance be watched for all of the daytime hours—which meant each of the two Nazi goons had to be sitting up in the woods for about seven hours at a time. He had them dress in dark green hunting gear so they would be

---

* Disappearing Act: As in a magic show, just seeming to disappear.
† Comings and goings: The people who visit, stay at, and leave a place.

more difficult to see. Schmidt made them climb a ridge to the steep hilltop spot he had selected. Almost a mile away from the castle, the site gave them *line-of-sight* coverage†* of the gate as well as the fronts of both the castle and the Vogels' cottage.

When the Vogels packed their old Volkswagen later in the day and drove away towards the west in the direction of Salzburg, Schmidt soon received the goons' report of their departure—this meant that half of his problem was solved. Schmidt now had to be concerned only about the Hales.

"Now it is a question of whether that *impolite‡* Dr. Hale and his dirty, potato-picking son and dog are going to be leaving as well. If so, we are much luckier than I would have thought possible. Maybe, after all, the coast will be *clear.§* And maybe I will not have to bother hurting or shooting anybody. I would not mind hurting Dr. Hale—in fact, if this were 1943 again, I would have shot him already. But, for now, I would rather we just get in and out of the castle without anyone seeing us, hearing us or knowing anything. The Fourth Reich depends on this!"

The second Nazi goon listened, eagerly nodded his head in agreement—as always—and said, "*Jawohl,§* Colonel"—as each Nazi goon always did.

The war had, of course, ended very badly for Nazi Germany which had not merely lost but had been crushed by the Allies.

---

*   Line-of-sight: A direct look at or view of the gate, not blocked by any trees.
†   Coverage: View.
‡   Impolite: Not polite, crude.
§   Coast will be clear: No one will be nearby and looking.
§   Jawohl: Pronounced 'Ya-vole' it means Yes Sir in the German military. It is a strong 'YES'.

The Fuehrer had killed himself as had SS Chief Heinrich Himmler and Marshall of the Reich Hermann Goering. Those were the most powerful monsters in Nazi Germany. The dreaded Russian Red Army now occupied much of Germany as well as a large chunk of Austria—the armies of the Americans and British occupied the rest. To make matters even worse, surviving SS and Gestapo officers like themselves were being hunted down like animals.

But, like the *fanatical** Nazis that they were, the former Gestapo and SS members pretended they were still in charge and dreamt of launching a Fourth Reich. Schmidt was getting restless to get back to the castle. The sun went down Thursday night, but there was still no *evidence*† that the Hales were going anywhere. All Schmidt had to *rely on*‡ was Dr. Hale's claim on the telephone that he would be leaving town. "What if he was lying just to get rid of me?" Schmidt mumbled. Impatient as ever, Schmidt grumbled again and yelled at his two goons to make sure they were back on the hillside at *daylight*§—"Early! If Hale leaves, you cannot miss it—or else."

As the Swiss clock in Matt Hale's study struck mid-night, Visitor tapped on the garden door. When Matt Hale welcomed him in, Visitor made his entrance *toting*⁋ a heavy carrying case. He was looking somewhat weary this time because he had not been to bed since getting the emergency meeting call the night

---

* Fanatical: Extremely devoted to a level most normal people would consider crazy.

† Evidence: Proof or facts to show that something is true.

‡ Rely on: Depend on.

§ Daylight: When the sun comes over the horizon and the area begins to brighten enough for one to see.

⁋ Toting: Carrying or hauling.

before. Since that time, he had been quite busy—the way intelligence officers *routinely** work. He not only had to get a hold of the correct explosive materials, but also *oversee*[†] creation of the *bogus*[‡] gold-lead bars.

And most importantly, he had received approval for this *deception operation*[§] that he and the Hales were putting together. At first, not everyone in the Intelligence Group *favored*[¶] the idea of letting the Nazis get away—much less do so with all the loot, fake or not. Some preferred setting a trap and arresting these monsters for murder. When Visitor pointed out that Dr. Hale's usefulness in intelligence operations would be all over—*kaput***—if the Nazis were arrested at his castle home, approval was given to go ahead with the plan proposed by Visitor and Dr. Hale. The Group agreed to let the Nazis go—but stick them with worthless lead bars, the fake British notes and travel documents with a *fatal*[††] weakness.

Why fatal? Because David Hale was photographing each and every one of them. In fact, these travel documents would prove useful to American Intelligence in tracking Nazi war criminals—for years to come—everywhere in the world! 'The Nazi 100' would become *marked men*[‡‡]—they would be *leaving footprints*,[§§] so to speak, when they used the fake names and

---

*   Routinely: Usually, on a regular basis, constantly.
†   Oversee: Manage and direct.
‡   Bogus: Fake or unreal.
§   Deception operation: A plan to fool an enemy by trickery.
¶   Favored: Liked.
**   Kaput: Finished, all over, hopelessly lost. From German 'kaputt'.
††   Fatal: Deadly.
‡‡   Marked men: Criminals well known to police around the world.
§§   Leaving their footprints: Like tracks in the snow, their travel documents would leave tracks that could be found and followed.

alias documents that Gestapo Chief Himmler had prepared for them. And such was the *genius** of the Hale plan that convinced the Intelligence Group to approve Matt Hale's plan of poisoning the well for almost 100 of the worst men on the planet—or at least those not already captured or dead.

Before Visitor left and took his usual path down to the river, Matt Hale told him he had come across something else in the lining of one of the trunks. He had found it only today. It was an old pre-war map of Austria from the 1930s. At first glance, it looked like any old country road map—but this one had some *discreet†* marks here and there that could mean something. He told Visitor he would photograph it after David finished copying the last of the travel documents. He added that he would have to reset the camera and lighting to copy the large map. The map itself would be going back into the trunk along with all the original Himmler materials—in case these *local‡* Nazis were expecting it to be there.

Finally, Matt said to Visitor that he was pleased at how well the gold-plated bars had come out. He said also he would probably not have noticed the reduced weight of the new mostly-lead bars if he had not recently handled the all-gold bars.

Visitor replied, "Maybe, Matt, we should go into gold mining some day—when the *Russian Bear§* has been caged. You know,

---

* Genius: Extremely smart, clever or intelligent.
† Discreet: Not too noticeable.
‡ Local: Near or close by; in this case, the three Nazis who have come sniffing around the castle.
§ Russian Bear: As the USA has the Bald Eagle as its national symbol, for Russia it has become the Brown Bear—although for much of the past century it was Russia's enemies who were using the Bear to show how big, slow to change, and brutal the Russians have been historically.

pure gold is indeed truly beautiful—like no other metal. Well, see you in Vienna on the weekend. Looks like we have a lot to do in that case too. *Gute nacht*."*

David had earlier finished up the photocopying of all the Nazi top-100 documents and pictures as Visitor headed out into the night. His dad was half expecting David to be physically drained and suggested the boy go upstairs and get some sleep "while I get the trunks and North Tunnel back into their original condition. Also, I need to set off this small bomb to blow some *debris*† around—so it looks normal to the Nazis when they come back."

As soon as David heard the word 'bomb,' he was *jolted*‡ wide awake. He now had no desire to *hit the sack*§ for some sleep. "Really, Dad, a bomb? That is fantastic. Can't wait. I'm not tired—not a bit!"

Dr. Matt Hale admitted he could use some help. So, again he led the boy to the kitchen and said, "Let's have a snack and a hot drink. It will take a while to close things up in the tunnel so it looks perfectly fine to the strangers when they dig their way in from outside—as I am pretty sure they will do. Breaking in through the outside wall will be quicker and more *secure*⁋ for them—less risky than getting trapped inside the castle." For the next hour, father and son—senior spy and junior spy—hauled the mass of materials back to the basement. All the while, Thor

---

*   Gute nacht: Good night in German.
†   Debris: Wreckage, ruins, litter or waste left after a storm, shipwreck or, as in this case, a bombing.
‡   Jolted: Shocked, shaken or stunned.
§   Hit the sack: Go to bed.
⁋   Secure: Safe.

kept watch just outside the burial chamber where Matt Hale had told him to stay.

Once everything was *in position*,[*] Matt Hale restored the trunks and the burial chamber—with David's very active help. It turned out that the boy was pretty gifted when it came to recalling the contents of each trunk—how it all looked earlier in the week when Thor had 'struck gold' in the castle tunnel. As the last trunk was shut, David turned to his pal and said, "Well Thor, as soon as we get done, I'm giving you a big chunk of beef. After all, without your great nose and without your digging, I would have walked away from all this. Good dog. Good boy. You're the best."

Still on duty and on patrol, Thor kept his eyes on the two skeletons—*reacting*[†] not at all to anything David was saying. Matt Hale was there and, to Thor, the father was obviously in charge. Matt Hale then re-blocked the tunnel. Within an hour, the explosion took place. It had the power only of a couple of *hand grenades*.[‡] The blast was enough to scatter a fair amount of dirt, rocks and dust—too little to damage the trunks or re-open the tunnel. Visitor, it seems, had been a *demolition expert*[§] in the war and knew just how much of an explosion was needed for this small task.

David and Thor were not deep in the tunnel, and David begged to sit on the cellar stairs so he could hear the blast.

---

[*] In position: In the correct or proper place.
[†] Reacting: Responding or showing some emotion when spoken to by the boy.
[‡] Hand grenades: Small explosive devices the size of a baseball and used in wartime combat.
[§] Demolition expert: Men who blow up bridges and other structures.

When he heard it explode, David chuckled—all he could say was "Holy smoke, Batman!"

Matt Hale waited a while to let the dust settle before he went back to see how things looked. He wore *surgical** glasses and a mask and carried David's two flashlights to be sure he could find his way back to the stairs in case one of the bulbs went out. After they *emerged*† from the cellar, Matt Hale said, "Let's get some sleep. The sun will be up in two hours and we have to pack. We're off to Vienna for a long, busy weekend. Well done, David, both you and Thor."

When the bomb went off, the North Tunnel rat population was stunned for the second time in two years. They again put several hundred feet between themselves and the explosion—between themselves and the bones of the Nazis who had fed them so well—once upon a time near the end of the war.

---

*   Surgical: The kind used by surgeons in a hospital when they are performing a medical operation.
†   Emerged: Came up from or out of.

14

Nazis Heading West

The Date: June 20, 1947—Friday.

The Hales packed the car in the morning for the drive into Vienna. Thor was going, too. David said to his dad that he was *itching** to sneak up to the parapet instead and keep an eye on things. "Too bad we can't see what happens," he added. "I wonder, Dad, if they will blow a big hole in the North Wall."

Matt Hale smiled at the boy and said, "I doubt they will explode anything. They probably just want to *retrieve*† their stuff and make a clean *getaway*.‡ But you're really thinking, Son. Anyway, things are under control—Visitor's team is taking care of that with some *long-distance*§ surveillance and photography. We will know who comes here, what car or cars they are driving, and when they have left Vienna. The three Hales including Thor, however, need to make a highly visible *departure*⁋ that shows the Nazis that the castle is absolutely empty—so they can make their break-in. So, let's get going."

As Matt Hale drove away from the castle, he kept his eyes on

---

* Itching: Anxious or badly wanting.
† Retrieve: Get back or recover.
‡ Getaway: An escape by criminals who want to avoid being captured by the police.
§ Long-distance: From quite far away, in this case a few hundred yards or maybe as much as a mile.
⁋ Departure: Exiting or leaving.

the road and made sure he and David avoided looking up into the hills where the Nazi's *O.P.** was located. The father knew the goons were in position to see him drive off in the direction of downtown Vienna. He wanted to leave the strangers feeling *smug*[†] and believing quite wrongly that they were in command of things. In fact, these leftover Nazis were *being played*[‡] and that gave Matt Hale some partial satisfaction.

Why only partial? Well, he too would like to have seen them captured breaking into the castle where the two murdered German soldiers lay buried inside the tunnel. This would have gotten them long prison sentences which they certainly deserved. But, arresting them would also bring public attention to Matt Hale, to his family, and to the castle—all that would serve no good purpose. Operating in the shadows—in the secret world of spies—was where he preferred to be as well as precisely where U.S. Intelligence officials in Vienna wanted him to remain. For it was there in clandestine operations that he could cause greater damage to old enemies—the Nazis—and to new enemies—the Russians. For *the time being*,[§] therefore, he would have to *settle for*[¶] giving this group of Nazi thugs false confidence that things were breaking their way.

And that was exactly how Schmidt later reacted when he received the team report that the castle was empty and that Dr. Hale and son had left. He was especially relieved to learn

---

* O.P. : Observation Post. Any high point or hidden spot that is used to watch the enemy.

† Smug: A feeling of too much or exaggerated confidence.

‡ Being played: When a person is being made the fool by those who are acting smarter.

§ The time being: For now or meanwhile; presently.

¶ Settle for: Accept and be satisfied with.

that the dog was gone, too. "Something about that animal really bothers me—didn't like him from the moment I first saw him."

Thor, for his part, had shown in their meeting at the castle gate how he felt about Schmidt. To the Hale's Patrol Dog, this Nazi was just like the enemy soldiers his handler Mike and he had fought and defeated on the battlefields of France and then Germany itself. Thor also had been shot by one of them. So, one might say, the bad feelings were *mutual** between Schmidt the German Nazi and Thor the German Shepherd. And, as is said about elephants, dogs too never forget—something Schmidt one day would find out.

David, meanwhile, had gone along with all of Dad's rules of the game this Friday morning. As much as he was itching to, he never once looked up into the hills where his father said the goons were hiding. He had also resisted the temptation to sneak up into the parapet and use his spyglasses to watch the Nazi watchers. Instead, he would follow Dad's orders and depart the castle without probably ever knowing how things turned out. It was the same, he thought, as reading through a Jack London adventure—*White Fang* for example—only to find deep into the story that someone had ripped the last chapter out of the book.

A slight breeze from the northwest drifted down the hillside to the road below. It carried the scent of the two former Nazi SS soldiers. As the Hale car slowly made its way along the curved bumpy road, Thor was in his favorite position—his head hanging out the rear window while he sniffed and pulled aromas in his usual canine way. Then, abruptly, he *converted*† from family

---

*   Mutual: The same for each of them.
†   Converted: Changed in an important way.

pet to the *stellar** Patrol Dog whose skills had taken him all the way from the beaches of Normandy in the great war. Thor came to attention and let out a low growl—he had picked up and recognized the familiar—but unpleasant—*whiff*[†] of nearby enemy troops. Knowing that Thor had picked up on the presence of *hostile*[‡] strangers, Matt Hale reached over to the back and stroked Thor's head, saying, "Okay, old boy, you can relax. This situation is under control."

When the goons saw the Hales leave, they returned to the hideaway where Schmidt was anxiously waiting. He was ready to get on with the dig. He had his goons load up the trunk of the Mercedes with the following: two shovels, two pickaxes, two sledge hammers, two sets of work gloves, and two wheelbarrows as well as paraffin lanterns. The two sets of this and that were for the goons—Schmidt had no intention of getting his hands dirty doing either the digging or the heavy lifting. After all, in his own mind he still was a senior Nazi SS Officer—war or no war—1943 or 1947!

As he drove up the road that led to the castle, Schmidt pulled into the field where Herr Vogel usually kept his cows. Driving deep into the *lush*[§] meadow, the Nazi came upon the small trail that would take them around to the north side of the castle. Arriving at the castle north wall, the goons unloaded the tools and began to dig. They could not be seen from the front road—they began working away believing wrongly that they could not be seen at all.

---

*   Stellar: Better than any other; a star animal; the best.
†   Whiff: A slight smell.
‡   Hostile: Enemy.
§   Lush: Rich and with a growth of new Spring grass.

Off in the distance, in fact, they were under *constant** surveillance as they had been from the moment they reached the
castle. Visitor had arranged with the U.S. Army to send two
special operations soldiers outfitted in *camouflage†* gear that
blended in with the *shrubbery.‡* The two American soldiers were
posted on a hilltop off to the northeast of the castle. As the
Nazi digging got underway, so did the US Army photography.

It was mid-morning when the digging got started. By noon,
they had made excellent progress. By mid-afternoon, they broke
through the outer stone wall to the inner chamber holding
two skeletons and the three-trunk treasure trove—the cache
that once held the prospect of getting these Nazis away from
Europe. They were eager to get away to a new part of the world
so they might start their evil Nazi business all over again. Junior
spy Hale, of course, took all those document photographs to
make the Nazis' prospects less promising and less likely to
succeed.

Once the wall was *breached,§* removing the trunks from the
tunnel took less time than Schmidt expected. By five o'clock
they were putting the dirt and stone back in place. All three
trunks were now in the back of the Mercedes. Because Schmidt
was too *arrogant§* to lift the trunks himself, he was never in a
position to detect whether the trunk with the fake 'gold bars'
felt heavy enough to be 'the real thing.' Within a few days he

---

*   Constant: Steady or non-stop.
†   Camouflage: Designs and markings on cloths, equipment and even
    buildings that makes a person or thing seem to not be there because
    the designs mix in with the trees and background.
‡   Shrubbery: Bushes, small trees and plant life.
§   Breached: Broken through.
§   Arrogant: Self-important; full of himself.

would wish he had not merely lifted that particular trunk but examined the 'gold bars' thoroughly.

Schmidt was feeling pretty good about things—humming a favorite SS marching song, in fact, as he drove away from 'his' wartime castle. He felt he had everything a runaway Nazi SS Officer and war criminal could dream of or hope for—a *documented** false identity and a Swiss passport to take him far away from Austria—far away from the hangman's noose. He now had plenty of money and 'gold' as well as a trunk filled with travel documents for former SS and Gestapo brutes who hoped to form the *nucleus†* of a Fourth Reich down in South America. All he had to do was get away from Vienna and follow the path to famously-*corrupt‡* Marseille—a French *port city§* barely seven hundred miles to the west of the Austrian capital. Schmidt could drive there in two days, three at the most.

The plan was then to get into Italy—that would not be difficult. All he would need to do was pay a *modest¶ bribe*** at the Italian border—by paying a bribe he would be warmly received by the *crooked††* border guard—*"Benvenuto en Italia."‡‡* He would cross into Italy at night when there was little traffic and less likelihood he would be spotted by anyone who knew

---

* Documented: With birth certificates and official papers that support a person's identification.

† Nucleus: In science it is the center of the atom; in this case, it means the center or heart of the new Nazi movement.

‡ Corrupt: Controlled by criminals.

§ Port city: A city from which ships travel to and from other cities around the world.

¶ Modest: Not too large and not too small.

** Bribe: A payment in money to get a person to let you do something dishonest or illegal.

†† Crooked: Dishonest.

‡‡ Benvenuto en Italia: "Welcome to Italy."

him or either of his two goons. They all would then drive down to the port city of Livorno and board an ocean *freighter** for Argentina. *Scores*[†] of wanted Nazi war criminals had gone there secretly since the war. Schmidt had also heard that the U.S. Military had recently closed its own Army base in Livorno which made him feel safer. Rather than a large city such as Marseille or even Rome, he had decided to leave Europe by boat from a small Italian port—he would be less likely to be caught there by American Nazi hunters who were a danger to war criminals like himself. Once he got into South America, he knew he would be protected.

---

* Freighter: An ocean-going ship that delivers goods all around the world and has a few passengers only.

† Scores: Many (literally groups of twenty), in this case hundreds.

15

Stopover in Salzburg—
Misery in Marseille

The Date: June 21–22, 1947

First, however, Schmidt had to take care of a few things. On
the way westward towards Marseille, he would make a brief
stopover.* He had arranged to meet with a *Neo-Nazi*† leader in
the Salzburg area, a little less than 200 miles west of Vienna.
Schmidt was anxious to *unload*‡ the trunk stuffed with travel
documents for the 'Nazi 100.' He also would pass along most
of the counterfeit British Five Pound Notes. It was not that
he was feeling generous. With the castle now occupied by an
American, he had no immediate safe place to hide anything so
bulky. He and his two goons could carry only so much *booty*§
with them on their trip out of Europe.

He was hopeful that the Neo-Nazis in Salzburg, in exchange
for the fake money and 'Nazi 100' travel documents, would do
something for him—maybe put him in contact with Marseille
criminals with whom he could deal safely and who'd be willing

---

*   Stopover: Staying for a day or so in a place during a longer journey.
†   Neo-Nazi: After the war, some wartime Nazis tried to create a secret
    Nazi movement and were called Neo-Nazis, or "New Nazis," although
    they were the same group of murderers who had just lost the war.
‡   Unload: Get rid of; pass on or transfer to.
§   Booty: Treasure.

to exchange *authentic** British money for the 'gold bars.' For Schmidt did not want to get stuck with 'Operation Bernard' bills or any other fake stuff. He was far too cautious for that.

At this point, Schmidt still believed his 'gold bars' were genuine. After all, the trunk with the four 'gold bars' though mainly lead—was pretty heavy. The bars had the Nazi Eagle stamped on them, and the entire shipment had been sent to him by SS Chief Heinrich Himmler himself. And, if he could not trust his dead Nazi cousin, who could Schmidt ever trust? So, he felt no urge to weigh or examine the bars carefully. The meeting with the Neo-Nazi leader in Salzburg went smoothly. It took place at the same spa where Schmidt was supposed to meet up with cousin Himmler two years earlier. That was when the Nazi empire was in collapse and the Fuehrer committed suicide in Berlin while the Russian Army closed in on his *bunker.*† The spa was owned and run by an old Nazi couple who were providing support to former war criminals on the run.

A *model*‡ of German *efficiency*,§ the Salzburg area Neo-Nazi leader—who called himself 'Karl' only—got immediately down to business. He was pleased to get hold of the fake British bank notes. What he really wanted and most gladly received, however, were the passports and travel documents for the 'Nazi 100.' Some of the top Nazi war criminals had been killed and others had been captured by the Allies and sentenced to death or prison. The least fortunate Nazis had been captured by

---

*   Authentic: Real, legitimate, not counterfeit.
†   Bunker: An underground hiding place that was strongly built.
‡   Model: Example.
§   Efficiency: Getting things done quickly and well; doing tasks effectively.

the Russians and executed immediately. It was done the usual Russian way—brutally, and with neither trials nor *witnesses*.* More than half of the fake travel documents were for escaped Nazis still hiding in Germany or Austria itself. Now, in control of these *precious*† papers, Karl's personal power within the Austria-Germany Neo-Nazi community was sure to increase. He was certain of that, for he knew that he alone now possessed the special ability to get leading Nazis safely away from Europe altogether.

The document review process took only an hour. They sat in a quiet, shady section of the garden enjoying a delicious Austrian meal that the proud Nazi innkeeper's wife had prepared for her 'important guests.' To an *uninformed*‡ observer watching from afar, they would have appeared to be a fine Austrian family and friends enjoying a simple social visit in the countryside. The difference between such a *serene*§ but false image and the violent monsters seated at that table could not have been greater. All had innocent blood on their hands and hatred in their hearts—wartime victims of this group numbered in the thousands.

When 'Karl' had finished his meal, he wrote out instructions and drew a map showing SS Col. Schmidt how and where to contact the Marseille criminals—most of them wartime Nazis now in the business of illegal drug trafficking. Drug dealing was a cash business, so it was expected that they would have

---

* Witnesses: Outsiders who knew of the killings.

† Precious: Valuable.

‡ Uninformed: Someone who did not know who these people really were.

§ Serene: Peaceful, quiet, friendly, harmless.

money *on hand** to exchange genuine British bank notes for 'gold.' They would not pay as high of an *exchange rate*† as a bank normally would pay—neither would they report Schmidt to the Allied officials who were always interested in catching former Nazi war criminals.

This was the safety Schmidt was seeking and would have gotten if the 'gold bars' had in fact been genuine. Criminal life, however, is quite often a dangerous road with many turns and unexpected changes of direction. As it turned out, Schmidt and his two goons drove after the lunch on to Marseille and contacted the criminals that 'Karl' had recommended. Everything seemed to be *on track*‡ and Schmidt was sure he would succeed in his escape.

The actual exchange for British money was set to occur alongside an old seaside lighthouse, not far from downtown Marseille. Being his usual cautious self, Schmidt ordered his goons to make the 'gold' delivery—he observed it all from a safe distant shore peering through his sniper scope. Schmidt kept his distance mainly because he did not want any of the criminals to be able to describe or identify him to the police later on.

He watched anxiously as his goons drove up to the lighthouse where a small truck and motorcycle were parked alongside. He watched as the waiting criminals removed the trunk from the back of Schmidt's car. This he expected. But, their next moves left him stunned. They quickly carried the

---

*   On hand: Available.
†   Exchange rate: The number of dollars or British pounds that one gets for another country's money.
‡   On track: Going according to plan.

trunk over to their own truck—a meat cutter's *scale** had been set up in the back. They then appeared to Schmidt to be weighing each of the four 'gold' bars. This got Schmidt's full attention—but did not concern him. After all, it occurred to him that this was a reasonable thing for them to do before paying for the 'gold' with real British money. Schmidt was still very much relaxed.

The next thing Schmidt witnessed, though, gave him an incredible surprise he was unprepared for and could hardly believe. His two goons were knocked to the ground by the thugs from Marseille. Each of Schmidt's men was then thrown into the back of the truck. He could see a hood being tied over the head of each man. Just as abruptly, the truck pulled away from the lighthouse and raced away from the harbor at full speed. All the *commotion*† took place in less than a minute—more like forty-five seconds—enough time for Schmidt's jaw to drop open—not long enough for him to even let out a sound.

Schmidt's first thought was not for the safety of his goons— instead, he was alarmed that he may have just lost 'his gold.' Fearful he too might be in danger, he immediately drove away by motorcycle and headed back to his small rented room. He needed to get hold of his travel documents and suitcase. *Momentarily*,‡ his thinking became *jumbled*§—he was alone—he was in shock. He frankly did not know what to do next. All through the war years, he and his castle goons had terrorized others. Now, in Marseille and with his goons gone, it was

---

* Scale: A machine used to weigh things.
† Commotion: Upset and violence.
‡ Momentarily: Briefly, for a short period of time.
§ Jumbled: All mixed up.

Schmidt who was terrified. He had also just lost his car—his favorite possession from the Third Reich!

Back in Vienna the following morning, American Embassy officials received a report that the bodies of two unidentified foreigners had washed ashore early that morning near Marseille. What made the news report so unusual—and *intriguing**—was that each drowning victim had a large melted chunk of lead in his mouth and throat. The police assumed they were Germans—each had the *Nazi SS Tattoo*† showing *blood type*‡ on his left arm. Rumors soon spread around criminal circles in Marseille that they had tried to sell lead-filled bars as though

*   Intriguing: Mysterious and unusual.

†   Nazi SS Tattoo: The 'Blutgruppentatowierung' was used in the German Nazi SS to show a soldier's blood type in case he was wounded in war and needed to be given a blood transfusion.

‡   Blood type: The particular kind of blood each person has—whether "A", "B", "AB", or "O".

they were solid gold. No one knew then, or would ever know, who they were. The castle goons had met the same *fate** as did tens of thousands of innocent Europeans whom the Nazis had made disappear in the war.

There was no mention in the news reports of a third person—it was the Embassy Intelligence Group's conclusion that Schmidt had probably escaped. If not, his body also would have been found. The Embassy felt they would *eventually*[†] know whether he had left for South America or remained in Europe. After all, the group was holding photos and passport numbers of all the travel documents David had photographed in the wee hours of the night—including Schmidt's.

Back in Marseille, it was Schmidt's turn to begin *analyzing*[‡] what happened—and why. He tried to contact 'Karl' in Salzburg by phone. The response he got was that 'Karl' was not available. 'Karl' had heard there was a problem with the "delivery" and now in fact, he too was being accused of trying to *pull a fast one*[§] on the Marseille gangsters. So, Neo-Nazi leader 'Karl' went into hiding and left a message for Schmidt not to contact him again any time soon.

Schmidt *re-read*[¶] the newspaper police report on the two drownings and rumors about 'fake gold.' This got Schmidt wondering—had Schmidt's own cousin shipped fake gold bars along with counterfeit British Bank Notes and false identity

---

*   Fate: Outcome, ending or result.

†   Eventually: Not right away but over the course of weeks or months.

‡   Analyzing: Thinking carefully and step by step about what may have happened with the Marseille gang.

§   Pull a fast one: Try to trick or fool someone with a clever move or deception.

¶   Re-read: Read over and over.

papers? If so, why hadn't SS Chief Himmler warned him in his 'most secret' message? And, if it was not Himmler, then who had done this to him? The Americans? Dr. Matt Hale?

Schmidt at this point was screaming in his hotel room like a *mad-man**—as he often had done in the war when things went badly. This time, however, there were no goons around to say "Jawohl, Colonel, Jawohl." The unlucky goons were gone.

Meanwhile, Visitor called for an emergency *safe-house*† meeting with Dr. Hale in downtown Vienna to tell him what was known about the drownings in Marseille. Matt Hale knew Schmidt might present a problem, but the doctor-spy was at the moment focused on pulling off an intelligence operation right under the noses of the Russian Secret Police. He had some casing to complete and little time to think—much less worry—about Schmidt or whether they would meet again. If he were to reappear, Matt Hale would deal with it. Like a solid chess master—in fact like a good spy. Matt Hale was always prepared to face unexpected things. He was quite *content*‡ to let the future work itself out. David, by contrast, had difficulty accepting the fact that—unlike the adventures he had read about in books—all things are not immediately knowable in the world of spies.

David was only beginning to see that occasionally spies quickly learn how matters work out—sometimes it takes a while—sometimes they never know. That is the *nature*§ of the spy world where secrecy and the unexpected play a larger role

---

*   Mad-man: An insane or crazy person.
†   Safe-house: A secret hideout where spies can meet without being seen or heard.
‡   Content: Happy or satisfied.
§   Nature: The way it is; how it really works.

than in most other fields or professions. It is, in fact, a major difference between *fiction** and *non-fiction,†* the make-believe and the real.

The boy looked over at Thor and whispered, "I have to become more like you, Old Boy. You don't seem to *fret‡* about yesterday things—I doubt you worry much about tomorrow. Heck, in some ways, you're more like Dad than I am. Imagine that, and I'm his son!"

The senior spy returned to the room and told David they were heading back to the castle for a few days. He said the Austrian *authorities§* and the Russians were *postponing‖* the conference a week as they argued about who was going to pay for and provide the food needed to run the event for five full days. The Russians had been continuing to remove great quantities of *produce*** from the local farms in their sector to feed the Red Army occupying most of Eastern Europe. Regardless of the change of schedule, Matt Hale by now knew where the Polish delegation would be staying. So, he would be ready to track down and *isolate††* Gorski to set him up for recruitment while the Polish officer was in Vienna. Now, the doctor spy could turn his attention back to the Nazi on the run, SS Col Schmidt and his family's security back at the castle.

---

* Fiction: Make believe stories or tales.
† Non-fiction: Real life stories or events.
‡ Fret: Be sorrowful or regretful.
§ Authorities: The Austrians who were in charge of running the country.
‖ Postponing: Making people delay or wait because things are not ready.
** Produce: Things grown on farms—vegetables, fruit, eggs and chickens, for example.
†† Isolate: Get Major Gorski alone so Visitor could speak with him privately without the Russians knowing.

16

Schmidt Chooses Revenge

The Date: June 23, 1947

As young David Hale—eleven going on twelve—sat high in the branches of the tall tree at the rear of the castle, he was feeling both content and *antsy*.* He was certainly happy that the Nazi plan to escape with all the loot had gone badly for them. But, he was not satisfied he had heard the end of it all. "Two down; one more to go" was how he put it in baseball terms to Thor, resting way down on the ground below. "Yeah, I am pitching in Yankee Stadium and have just struck out the first two batters— ninth inning—American League 1947 Pennant on the line. But I still have to face 'Jolting Joe' DiMaggio. Now everything is *at stake*.† So I ask my catcher, 'Thor, do I throw him fast balls or curves? Inside or out? High or low?'" Well this time 'coach' Thor was no help at all—he was too busy scratching himself.

David, of course, was trying to figure things out here in Vienna if the tall German returned—not what to do in an imaginary game on the baseball diamond back in New York. What the young spy was doing was thinking ahead and pre- paring himself in case Schmidt actually returned. David looked long and hard at Thor, finally smiled and said, "Heck, Thor, I

---

* Antsy: A little worried or concerned.
† At stake: On the line and at risk.

have my answer—you are my *ace in the hole** and with you at my side, I have a special partner and ally. I feel better already."

The day had gotten started early. Dr. Hale had to drive north a hundred miles to the refugee hospital in Linz and spend the entire day there. The late-night call he had received concerned another outbreak of cholera as well as typhus—both probably caused by a new wave of displaced persons arriving from nearby Czechoslovakia. Before leaving the castle gate this morning, the senior spy had spoken with both Konrad and Katrina Vogel to be on the lookout for Schmidt. He gave them a *summary†* of the events in Marseille and that two of the recent castle visitors had been drowned; the third was probably very much alive and quite dangerous. The Vogels said they would be ready if he indeed showed up at the gate with any more fake stories about old friends and such. Both Vogels, husband and wife—with their wartime secret service in the Underground Army—were quite experienced with guns and dealing with Nazis. They assured Dr. Hale that they would be ready and keep David safe as if he were their own son.

SS Col. Schmidt, *unemployed‡* since Germany lost the war, had just arrived back in Vienna from Marseille. This was the first time in a *decade§* that he was operating entirely alone now that his two goons were not only unemployed, but dead. So, there was no one to ask Schmidt why he had not just boarded the boat leaving Livorno, Italy for South America within a

---

*   Ace in the hole: An extra card in a game of poker and in this case an extra ally or partner.

†   Summary: A brief explanation.

‡   Unemployed: Out of work.

§   Decade: Ten year period.

week. He still had his Swiss passport, enough money and his ticket for the voyage. He likely would reach Argentina before British or American authorities learn he had left Europe. Once away from the Nazi-hunters around Europe, war criminals had hundreds of places in the Andes Mountain range to hide as Nazis had been doing since 1944. Schmidt had heard very good things about Chile and Peru—he liked the mountains.

As he sat on his motorcycle-with-sidecar and, looking up at the castle from a distance, he finally asked himself the same question. "Hey, Schmidt, why not just drive away, head back to Italy and get on the ship? Our SS network in South America is strong and will help you while building the foundation for our new 'Fourth Reich.' The new Reich will be *enormously** advanced in super weapons this time. The Americans are not the only ones who can design atomic bombs and we Germans are very far ahead in missiles."

But, Schmidt found none of these good enough reasons for him to leave Austria immediately. He now realized it was personal *revenge*[†] he wanted most of all. He ached inside to strike back at the Americans—especially at Dr. Hale who had left him hanging on to a silent or dead telephone a couple of weeks earlier. Even his goons had *smirked*[‡] as he stood there burning in anger. "It has to be Hale," he grumbled. "He stole my gold—he stuck me with the lead-filled junk. And, he is going to pay for this. Yes, I will shoot the boy and dog first—then Dr. Hale. Revenge is funny—just thinking about it feels good."

---

*   Enormously: Greatly.

†   Revenge: Getting even with an enemy by doing something bad to them.

‡   Smirked: Smiling when trying not to.

He moved in nearer to the castle, to the same hill and spot his goons had used days before. It was almost dusk and the old Nazi decided to enter the castle and get both his revenge and his gold by midnight. He would sail, after all, to South America a rich not a poor Nazi, a happy not a miserable one. Though he did not personally miss his goons, he did miss having soldiers to boss around and who could do any heavy lifting.

By nine o'clock that evening, Schmidt was already up behind the castle on the north side, which brought him in close to the tower. He had a flashlight and his Luger in case they were needed. For former SS Colonel Schmidt, this was indeed a military operation. He even wore his old *combat boots** and the *Nazi Iron Cross*[†] his cousin awarded him for stealing so much Austrian artwork. In Schmidt's mind, the evening would end with either him or Hale victorious. He was not interested in doing this half way or any other way. "Kill or be killed."

The *aging*[‡] Nazi did not look like any *historic*[§] German warrior. He was breathing heavily after crawling and climbing through so much underbrush on the castle hillside. Two years of sitting around drinking beer and eating rich Bavarian food since the war had turned him into an overweight, *inflated*[¶] copy of himself. He had barely been able to squeeze into his combat gear. Schmidt looked as though he was wearing another man's uniform. He felt that way, too. All the same, his heart was as

---

*   Combat boots: Heavy footwear worn by soldiers fighting out in fields and streams.

†   Nazi Iron Cross: A German medal given to soldiers for bravery in battle.

‡   Aging: Getting older for a soldier.

§   Historic: Famous from history.

¶   Inflated: Swollen and looking like he was filled with air.

fiery as ever—despite the extra fifty pounds of weight, he had fourteen years of Nazi hate running through his veins.

Yes, from the day in 1933 when Adolf Hitler became Chancellor and leader of Germany, Schmidt awoke each day and fell asleep each night with one thing in mind—conquer our enemies so that Germany alone would rule the world. "Yes," he thought, "with superweapons and hideouts in the mountains of South America, we Nazis could destroy America-England-Russia. Yes, we can still win the war and have our final victory."

Right now, of course, he had a job to do—recover the gold! Even that much gold would not be enough, but Schmidt also had the secret map his cousin had hidden in the lining of the last trunk. It was a map of Austria with marks showing in which salt mines the SS had hidden the artworks and jewelry Himmler had *assembled** through the Vienna Castle group. Himmler's stolen art was as good and valuable as Hitler's and Goering's stolen collections *combined*.† Schmidt and his men began hiding it on June 7, 1944—a day after the Allies landed on the beaches in Normandy, France.

Under Himmler's orders, while the entire Nazi Army fought for ten long months to defend Germany from the invading Allies—Americans, British, Polish, Canadians and French attacking from the West—the Russian Red Army attacking from the East—Himmler's Gestapo was busy hiding stolen art treasure for their own survival after the war. Much of the stolen art had—like the castle itself—been taken from murdered Jews.

---

*   Assembled: Gathered or pulled together after stealing them from innocent people and museums.

†   Combined: All together.

Back to the job at hand, Schmidt came alongside the small door leading to the castle kitchen and backstairs. He reached down to a bush to the right of the door and picked up a rock the size of a large potato. Turning it over, he was glad to see in the hollowed-out rock the brass key he had placed there two years earlier. It was still encased in *putty** and as good as new—once he scraped away the dried-out putty. He inserted the key in the old back door. The lock turned freely.

Schmidt chuckled thinking that the careless American Dr. Hale had not yet changed every lock in the castle—especially the lock on this old kitchen door. Well, Hale indeed had found that key—he left it there to be sure he and David would know which door the German would use if he tried to get back inside. As far as Hale's emergency *evacuation*[†] plan was *designed*,[‡] SS Col. Schmidt was coming in the correct way. David could, therefore, use a different way out—through the third floor window and roof leading out to the Parapet. The senior Hale knew from experience that David and Thor often departed that way when in a great hurry or if the boy did not want to be seen on the castle stairs.

Konrad Vogel was told about this plan and was prepared to see that, if the uninvited German got inside the castle again, it would be the last time—the only time. For Matt Hale and the Vogels, this was a leftover chapter in the Second World War and Schmidt was just another leftover Nazi killer and war criminal.

---

*   Putty: Soft wet material like clay used in building homes and putting glass in windows.

†   Evacuation: An escape path for leaving a building or place to avoid danger.

‡   Designed: Built in a careful, detailed way.

David, meanwhile, was as wide awake as Schmidt. His dad had telephoned on the drive back from Linz to say he would be late getting home. There had been a traffic accident a few miles south of Linz and, as the only doctor driving that way, he stopped to help those hurt in the crash. Fortunately, it was in the American and not the Russian Sector so a U.S. Army ambulance was on its way. But, Dr. Hale knew, he would not arrive back in Vienna till after mid-night. He reminded David to stay alert and follow the plan if anything unusual took place. The boy assured his dad he would.

Schmidt was sneaking awkwardly around the kitchen area and back stairs. He had spent little time in that part of the castle during the war. He once was, after all, Commander of that SS Unit—not one of the foot soldiers like his goons. Having concluded that there were no Hales on the ground floor, Schmidt started climbing the back stairs, on his way to the second floor.

When the German's heavy boot pressed down on the creaky third stair, David knew what was going on—what he had to do. He dropped out of bed and *scooted** over to Thor and whispered, "Old Boy, time to go—up and out." The two very *practiced†* night-time wanderers glided into the front hall and started silently up the staircase leading to the third floor and window out to the roof and Parapet beyond. The original *expectation‡* was that the doctor-spy would be home and inside the castle if Schmidt made his visit—in that case Senior Spy Matt Hale would be there to greet and deal with him. But,

---

*   Scooted: Moved quickly.
†   Practiced: Trained after having done it many times before.
‡   Expectation: What they believed would happen.

with the doctor stuck on the road back from Linz, the *back-up plan** was that Konrad Vogel would go into action—do what had to be done.

Schmidt meanwhile was ascending the back stairs ever so slowly—his feet hurt, he was not used to the dark, his over-stuffed belly meant he could barely fit on the narrow staircase designed centuries earlier for smaller, *leaner†* people. By the time Schmidt reached David's bedroom, the boy and Patrol Dog were already out the third floor window onto the roof. They quickly but carefully made their way over to the Parapet where David crouched down low behind the tower wall. He then removed from his carrying sack the Army flashlight and old army sock to signal Konrad Vogel.

The old Austrian freedom fighter was in position on an *elevated‡* hunting stand that gave him a clear moonlit view of the parapet as well as the entire south side of the castle—including the hallway window next to David's room. He spotted David's signal. Vogel had gone there earlier in the evening when Dr. Hale called to say he would be late. Vogel was holding his freshly-cleaned *Mauser K98§* which was one of the best infantry rifles of the war and a real favorite of the German Army—especially its *snipers.¶*

At precisely ten o'clock the Nazi made his move. He climbed

---

*   Back-up Plan: What would be done if the situation changed.

†   Leaner: Thinner.

‡   Elevated: Several feet off the ground; up in the air.

§   Mauser K98: A bolt-action rifle adopted in 1935 as the standard service rifle by the Germans. It remained their primary service rifle until the end of the war in 1945.

¶   Snipers: Soldiers who are extremely good at shooting enemy from long distances.

the stairs up to the third floor. He saw the open window leading out onto the roof. Just as Matt Hale had expected and planned for, Schmidt began climbing out onto the roof, hoping to catch the boy and dog in the parapet. He had figured out by then that Dr. Hale was not there. So he decided he would get his revenge on the American doctor by shooting the boy and his dog. He took his Luger in his right hand as he climbed out the window. Maybe, he thought, he would shoot his victims and get out of there so he could catch that ship heading for South America. After all, he would have gotten his revenge—but right now he was more than a little afraid.

Suddenly, things went quite badly for Schmidt—he lost his grip on the window sill and went *cascading** down and off the roof like a walrus falling off an iceberg. The Luger flew through the air. To the old Nazi, it seemed that his *plunge*† through the bright Vienna night sky lasted forever—a lifetime, really. But, later on, the laws of *physics*‡ told David that, at thirty-two feet per second, the fall itself lasted maybe three, no more than four seconds, before Schmidt crashed hard on the rocks below. This Nazi who had terrorized others in the war screamed all the way down—louder than any of his many wartime Austrian victims.

What would have happened if he had not fallen to his death? Konrad Vogel, in keeping with the plan, was a couple of seconds away from firing off a *round*§ from his Mauser K98. He had

---

*   Cascading: Tumbling out of control.
†   Plunge: An awkward fall through the air or into deep water.
‡   Physics: The science and laws of motion, heat, light and forces that control the planets and the universe.
§   Round: A bullet or shot from a rifle or pistol.

Schmidt in his sights—Konrad was ready to *pull the trigger** as he had done in combat against the Nazis many times in the war. Now, with Schmidt as dead as the two goons found floating in Marseille, Vogel had only to clean up the Schmidt mess, put him on a raft, and float him *downstream*† to the Danube River that would take him on to the Black Sea, hundreds of miles to the south.

Before pushing Schmidt away from shore, Vogel unclipped the Iron Cross and SS stripe from the Nazi's uniform, placed them in Schmidt's mouth, and sent him on his way. Anyone finding the body would thereby know what they had found— one of the German monsters who had cost the Austrians 250,000 soldiers and over 100,000 *civilians*‡ killed in WWII.

Schmidt, of course, never would get to Argentina, the Andes Mountains of South America, or to any more pleasant meals with Neo-Nazis around Salzburg. Nor would he be able to support the Fourth Reich *fantasy*§ that he and other German war criminals thought they could build. In many ways, the leftover Nazis were quite like the rats *scurrying*⁋ around the dark cellar tunnels of the Vienna castle. They were not going to recover. They were going nowhere. The very good *outcome*** was that David Hale was safe, castle Security and Cover had been *maintained*†† and Austria was rid of another Nazi who brought only pain and death to this beautiful nation.

---

*   Pull the Trigger: Fire the rifle and shoot a bullet.
†   Downstream: The direction toward which a river or stream flows. Opposite of upstream.
‡   Civilians: People not serving in the military.
§   Fantasy: A foolish or not realistic dream or wish.
⁋   Scurrying: Running without any clear goal.
**   Outcome: Result or what happened.
††   Maintained: Kept or protected.

By the time Dr. Hale arrived back to the castle it was shortly after midnight and everything was *tranquil** as it was when he had left for Linz twenty hours earlier. He was surprised at this late hour to see so many lights were still on and to find David chatting with Konrad Vogel down at the castle gate. Thor was there as well. It didn't take long for Vogel to fill in the doctor on how things had developed that evening—Schmidt was *no more*[†] and that was what interested Matt Hale the most. The trap set for Nazi Colonel Schmidt did not *unfold*[‡] exactly as he had expected it would. Schmidt, after all, had fallen to his death. But, as far as Hale was concerned, and as Shakespeare wrote, "*All's well that ends well.*"[§] With Schmidt floating miles away from the Vienna castle, the Hales were no longer in danger.

David and Thor finally climbed the stairs back up to bed. David looked over at Thor and said, "Well, old pal, that was Strike Three!" Yes, the last Nazi was now dead. Before dozing off, the boy tried to decide which adventure made him feel better—getting the Polish scientist to freedom in the West, or blocking the escape to South America by Nazis with the documents, money and gold? When he couldn't *reach a conclusion,*[¶] David Hale just drifted off into a deep and peaceful night's sleep. More adventure lay just ahead. Next time, again, it would be against the Russians.

---

*   Tranquil: Peaceful and quiet.
†   No More: Dead.
‡   Unfold: Happen.
§   All's Well That Ends Well: A play written by English writer and poet William Shakespeare. It means that what really matters is how things finish up, the final result.
¶   Reach a conclusion: Decide or come up with an answer that made sense to him.